RANDOM HOUSE

LARGE PRINT

BOMBSHELL

STUART WOODS
AND PARNELL HALL

RANDOM HOUSE
LARGE PRINT

BOMBSHELL

All rights reserved.
Published in the United States of America by Random House Large Print in association with G. P. Putnam's Sons, an imprint of Penguin Random House LLC.

Cover illustration © Mike Heath

Halftone dotted background © sergio34/shutterstock.com

The Library of Congress has established a Cataloging-in-Publication record for this title.

ISBN: 978-0-593-28604-3

www.penguinrandomhouse.com/large-print-format-books

FIRST LARGE PRINT EDITION

Printed in the United States of America

10 9 8 7 6 5 4 3 2 1

This Large Print edition published in accord with the standards of the N.A.V.H.

BOMBSHELL

1

eddy Fay woke up to the sound of breaking glass. He grabbed the remote control from the nightstand and clicked on the monitor of the high-tech security system Mike Freeman had installed in his house. A dozen views appeared showing the exterior, a red dot pinpointing the source of the break-in. Another click of a button and the image moved to fill the screen; Teddy could see a burly man attempting to get through the living room window. He was being thwarted by a second pane of glass that was far sturdier than the one he'd just broken.

Teddy grabbed a gun, slipped down the stairs,

out a side door, crept up on the man, and jabbed the gun in his back.

The man whirled around and lunged for the gun.

Teddy groaned. Really? If Teddy had wanted to shoot him, the man would be dead. A mere burglar wouldn't take that chance. Was he a hired assassin, or just dumb?

Teddy spun around and chopped down on the man's arm. The intruder howled in pain, but he wasn't done. He shoved his wounded hand into his pocket and came out with a snub-nosed revolver.

Teddy almost felt sorry for him. The man's hand was numb, and he could hardly hold the gun. Teddy batted it away.

Three armored security vans roared up the driveway. A squad of Strategic Services agents poured out, guns drawn.

"Relax, gentlemen," Teddy said. "The situation seems to be in hand."

A young agent who appeared to be in charge said, "You're Billy Barnett?"

"At your service."

"Your system registered a security breach. Is this the intruder?"

"That he is."

"We'll be happy to take him off your hands."

"I doubt if you'll have him long. The system is also linked to the police. I believe that's them now."

A police car came up the drive with its red and blue lights flashing. A uniformed officer climbed out of the driver's seat, surveilled the scene, and said laconically, "What's all this?"

"Attempted B and E," Teddy said. "I'm the homeowner. That's the intruder. These gentlemen are private security guards who responded to my alarm."

The officer turned to the agent. "You apprehended the intruder in the attempt to break and enter?"

The agent shook his head. "The homeowner apprehended the intruder."

"Before you got here?"

"That's right."

The cop turned back to Teddy. "So you're the only witness to the attempted break-in?"

"Aside from the alarm system he activated."

"There's no evidence **he** activated the alarm system."

"Actually, there is. This is a Strategic Services system, with all the bells and whistles, including cameras. Here, take a look." Teddy led the officer over to the front door. "The main control is in the master bedroom, but this is the downstairs terminal." He pointed to a screen on the wall, and activated the control panel beneath it. An image immediately appeared on the screen, along with a graphic that read: FRONT LEFT WINDOW. The intruder had just smashed the outer window and was going to work on the inner. As the cop watched, he could see Teddy creeping up on the intruder and handily disarming him.

"There you are, Officer," Teddy said. "As you can see, it was an armed B and E. I'll give you a thumb drive of the video for evidence."

"You have a gun?"

"I have a permit for it."

"Good. Bring it down to the station with you, and you can swear out a complaint."

Teddy glanced at his watch. "I'll drop by later. Right now I've got a party to go to."

"A party? It's four in the morning."

"Yeah, the party's at five." Teddy smiled. "Good thing the guy woke me up. I might have been late."

It was still dark when Teddy pulled his 1958 D Model Porsche Speedster to a stop in front of Peter and Hattie Barrington's house. He skipped up the front steps and rang the bell.

Peter Barrington opened the door. "Come in, the gang's all here. The TV's on and they're about to start."

"Relax. It's the technical awards first. They don't get to the real thing until five-thirty."

"I'll be sure to tell lighting and set design what you think of them," Peter said dryly.

Teddy followed Peter out onto the veranda, where Hattie was sitting with Ben and Tessa.

Peter's wife, Hattie, was a gifted composer and

pianist, and had scored Peter's latest movie, among others.

Ben Bacchetti was the head of the studio. He was also Peter's best friend of many years. Their fathers, Stone Barrington and Dino Bacchetti, were also best friends.

Tessa Tweed Bacchetti had come to the studio as an aspiring young actress. She was now a star, and Ben Bacchetti's wife.

Teddy had been in England for Peter and Hattie and Ben and Tessa's double wedding. The young newlyweds were only partly aware of the role he had played in seeing that it went off without a hitch.

"There he is," Tessa said. "I told you he'd be here."

"Sorry I'm late," Teddy said. "Someone tried to rob me."

"Rob you?" Ben said.

Teddy shrugged. "Rob me or kill me, I'm not sure which. The police are asking him now."

Tessa grinned. "Would you stop being so maddeningly casual? You may take these things in stride, but robbing and killing are not really that routine."

"Well, I certainly hope to learn more about it, but the police have taken it out of my hands. The burglar couldn't get through Mike Freeman's security system, but he sure set off enough alarms. The poor guy never knew what hit him."

"I'll bet," Ben said.

"But don't let me spoil Oscar nominations morning. I was just explaining why I was late."

"The only thing that could spoil this Oscar morning," Hattie said, "is having a nervous breakdown waiting for it."

"Who's nervous?" Peter said. "No one's nervous."

"No one, I'm sure." Hattie smiled teasingly. "Has anyone else noticed who hasn't sat down once since everyone arrived?"

"I'm the host," Peter said. "I'm greeting my guests."

"I can attest to that," Teddy said. "I arrived. He greeted me. He was a little concerned by my tardiness, but I wouldn't characterize it as being nervous."

Peter put up his hands. "Yes, yes, we can all play it cool. But it is the Oscars. Before they get going, let me say this."

Peter took a breath. "I think it's great we could get together this morning to celebrate our film. But while awards are nice, that's not why we do this. We're not out to win awards, only to make good movies. If we can do that, and turn out a film we can be proud of, we don't need outside validation. We know we've done a good job. You all know how I feel about you, and awards or not, I'm very pleased with how this all turned out."

"Well, that's gracious and self-deprecating," Ben said with a grin. "In case you don't remember, your picture just won a Golden Globe. An Oscar nomination is not such a long shot."

"It won for Best **Drama**," Peter said. "At the Globes you're only competing with half the films. There's a strong field of comedies this year."

Hattie laughed. "Would someone nominate him already, before this naysayer ruins the whole party?"

Hattie got the first nomination for Best Original Score. The announcement was cause for jubilation. Hattie had been passed over by the Golden Globes. Peter had reassured her that the Golden Globe voters weren't necessarily the most knowledgeable of the category, and Oscar voters would know better. He was delighted to have been proven right.

"What did I tell you?" Peter said.

"Oh, God," Hattie said. "Now we're going to have to listen to him take credit for my nomination all morning."

Peter had his own nominations to brag about. He scored two, for Best Original Screenplay and Best Director.

Finally they got to the acting categories. Best Supporting Actor was first. Stuntman character actor Mark Weldon got a nod for his turn as villain Leonard Kirk.

"Too bad he's not here," Teddy said, and everyone laughed.

There was a tense moment when they got to Best Actress. None of the first four names were Tessa Tweed. For the first time all morning, the room was deathly quiet.

"And Tessa Tweed," the announcer said, "for **Desperation at Dawn**."

The announcement was met with relief, laughter, and applause.

"Told you so," Teddy said

"You realize this ups her price for your next film," Ben kidded Peter.

Peter smiled. "What are you telling **me** for? You're head of the studio."

"Oh, hell."

After all that, it was almost an anticlimax when the film was nominated for Best Picture.

3

On the other side of town, Viveca Rothschild, dubbed the Blonde Bombshell by the press, was hosting a similar Oscar party. Twenty-nine, lithe, blonde, and voluptuous, Viveca had already racked up two nominations in her career, but she had never won. After a lifetime of playing femmes fatales, her departure role in a romantic comedy had been a gamble, but it had paid off. Dancing, singing, and delivering big laughs, she had wowed the critics with her versatility, earning her best reviews ever. After taking home her first Golden Globe for Best Actress in a Musical or Comedy, an Oscar nomination was all but assured.

Viveca couldn't have been more nervous. Only the presence of her Hollywood friends and her boyfriend, Bruce, were helping her hold it together. Or at least put up the appearance.

On the television, the presenter said, "The nominations for Best Screenplay are . . ."

The announcement was met by boos, hisses, and catcalls.

Viveca's best friend, Cheryl, threw a napkin at the screen. "How many damn categories are there?" she said, and everyone laughed.

"Don't worry, honey," Bruce said. "I know you're going to be nominated."

Viveca put up her hand tolerantly, urging her boyfriend to be quiet. Bruce was a handsome young man with rippled muscles and a charming smile, and had been her high school sweetheart. But he was not good at picking up on social cues. Bruce had been wounded in Iraq and had come home with a Purple Heart, a Medal of Honor, and the resultant post-traumatic stress disorder. For the most part he had a pleasant nature, but as far as his girlfriend was concerned, he was ready to fly to her defense at the slightest provocation.

The screenwriting nominations gave way to Best Director.

"Did anybody act in these movies?" Cheryl said, and everybody laughed.

As if he heard her, the presenter said, "And the nominees for Best Supporting Actress are . . ."

"**Supporting!**" Cheryl wailed. "Kill me now!"

Finally they got to Best Actress. Three names were read, none of them Viveca's. Fourth time was the charm.

"Viveca Rothschild, for **Paris Fling**."

The entourage burst into roars of approval.

"Quiet, quiet!" Viveca said. "One more to go!"

The room was instantly hushed, with everyone thinking the same thing.

Viveca murmured it under her breath: "**Not** Meryl Streep! **Not** Meryl Streep!"

"And Tessa Tweed, for **Desperation at Dawn**," the presenter said, and the room collectively sighed in relief.

Viveca had dodged that one last bullet.

An Oscar was within her grasp.

Chaz Bowen eyed the attorney suspiciously. He had no reason to. The attorney, Richard Fitzgerald, was a slick shyster who represented a number of mobsters and crime bosses in the Los Angeles area. Which was exactly the type of lawyer Chaz needed, only Chaz was too dumb to know it.

Chaz was a sullen man, with hostile eyes, who suspected no one liked him. He was not entirely wrong on that count.

"Who the hell are you?"

"I'm your attorney, Mr. Bowen. I'm here to get you out."

"Well, you took your time getting here," Chaz snarled.

"You made the mistake of getting arrested in the middle of the night. The system works slower then."

"Can I go home?"

"What'd you tell the cops?"

"Told 'em I wanted a lawyer."

"Anything else?"

"Hell, no."

"You didn't try to give them a reason why you were trying to break into a Hollywood producer's house?"

"Couldn't think of one. Can you?"

"So what happened?"

"How the hell should I know? A simple break-in and a fucking SWAT team shows up. What the hell is that all about?"

Fitzgerald went out and hunted up Jason Rollins, the assistant district attorney assigned to the case.

"Hey, Jason. Wanna play **Let's Make a Deal**?"

"Ricky Fitz. How the hell are you?"

"Pissed, that's how. I was up at the crack of dawn to come down here just to bail a guy out."

"What's the case?"

"Chaz Bowen."

"Oh, that one. Slam dunk. Caught in the act

with burglar tools and a gun. Breaking into a Hollywood producer's house, for Christ's sake."

"Was he arrested in the house?"

"He was apprehended while trying to get in the window."

"So you can't charge him with breaking and entering. He didn't enter."

"I can charge him with attempted burglary."

"You'll never get a conviction."

"Give me a break. You're going to cop a plea and you know it. You can't put that guy in front of a jury. If he answers questions, he's guilty. If he refuses to answer questions, he's guilty. The minute he steps into court, he's guilty."

"My client doesn't want to serve time."

"Then he shouldn't have gotten arrested."

"I couldn't agree more. Shall we pretend he didn't?"

"Unfortunately he's been booked."

"You can always drop the charges."

"With so much evidence? My boss would want to know why. His-lawyer-told-me-to is a very poor answer."

"I gotta get him out."

The ADA shook his head. "You cop a plea, he's doing time. I can't give you a deal where he doesn't."

"How about time served?"

"A half an hour? Come on, Ricky, the charge isn't going away. The only way he's gets out is on bail."

"How much?"

Donnie Martel snatched up the phone. "Yeah?"

"Donnie. Rick Fitzgerald. You sent me to bail out Chaz."

"Did you do it?"

"Sure thing."

"How much?"

"Hundred thousand."

"That much?"

"The guy had a gun on him, Donnie. He's lucky he's out at all."

"Did he talk?"

"If he had, he'd have talked himself into a cell. The guy's a moron, Donnie. Shutting up is the only bright thing he's ever done."

"Are you kidding me? The guy's an expert locksmith."

"That is the type of thing I don't want to know, Donnie."

"Why didn't he talk?"

"He couldn't think of anything to say."

"Jesus."

....

Donnie slammed down the phone. Donnie Martel was a lower-level crime boss with big aspirations and little to show for it. He was always eager to do jobs for the big boys, the shit jobs that no one wanted to do but everyone needed done. He did a lot of them, and most of them panned out. When they came off without a hitch, they were completely unappreciated. No one ever noticed his efforts until something got fucked up. In Donnie's case it was always baby steps forward, and a gigantic slide back.

Chaz Bowen was one hell of a slide. The situation couldn't have been worse. Here he was, doing a job for the one guy on the West Coast he wanted to impress. Gino Patelli was the big boss, the legit boss, the one the others all kowtowed to, the one who was never personally involved in anything.

Donnie couldn't believe it had all gone wrong. It had been such a simple job. Yes, it was a hit, but it was an easy hit, not like whacking some rival mob boss. It was a movie producer, for God's sake, Mr. John Q. Public. This wasn't a complicated scenario, it was supposed to have been just a home invasion gone bad. The stupidest thug in the world should have been able to pull that off.

But no, Donnie had to find one even stupider.

So now he had to tell Gino Patelli that the simple assignment the big man had condescended to give him had blown up in his face.

Donnie picked up the phone to make the call. He started punching in the number, but found his hand was shaking. He slammed down the receiver.

Damn.

This would have to be done in person.

5

Gino Patelli's mansion might have belonged to a movie star. Many of the homes in Bel-Air did. Few belonged to crime bosses. Such clientele were discouraged, but Gino Patelli passed muster on two counts. First, he presented himself as a vintner, and while this pretense fooled no one, it was hard to dispute, since he owned enough vineyards to have stocked every tavern on the West Coast. In fact, he barely produced enough wine for his own table, and couldn't care about the rest. Still, it gave him bragging rights on the one hand, and a legitimate front on the other.

The other thing that made Gino Patelli hard to ignore was the fact that people were afraid of him.

Men who crossed him fell upon hard times. Cause and effect was always hard to prove.

Donnie Martel rang the buzzer at the iron gates, and identified himself for the camera mounted there. He wasn't asked his business. He was not getting in unless his business was already known.

After a few moments, the massive gates swung open. Donnie drove up the long, tree-lined drive, and parked in the circle in front of the mansion. He got out and went up to the front door. He could practically feel the X-ray from the scanner checking him for a weapon.

The door was opened by two silent goons who double-checked the scanner and patted him down for a gun. Finding none, they turned him over to a nondescript man in a faded suit with a paisley tie who looked like he couldn't hurt a fly. Donnie knew better. Sylvester was Gino Patelli's right-hand man. People who crossed Gino had a habit of disappearing. Sylvester was rumored to be the reason why.

Sylvester walked Donnie down the long, wood-paneled hall to the double-doored office at the end. Another goon patted him down again before opening the door.

Donnie took a breath and followed Sylvester in. The door closed behind him. Donnie had to fight the impulse to look back. He and Sylvester stepped up and stood in front of the large oaken desk.

Gino Patelli was young for a crime boss, particularly one of such prominence. He came into power on the death of his uncle, Carlo Gigante. For Gino it had been a rude awakening. The young Patelli was a ne'er-do-well playboy with a weakness for drinking, gambling, and loose women. His father had died shortly after he was born. His uncle raised him and spoiled him rotten, while teaching him the family business. For young Gino it was the ideal situation. He had all of the experience with none of the responsibility.

With Carlo Gigante's death, Gino was suddenly thrust into power. He took to it with a vengeance, and soon began bossing everyone around unmercifully. His meanness enhanced his standing. He was a bad man to disappoint.

Donnie shifted from one foot to the other. Gino had not looked up from his desk. Donnie knew better than to open his mouth before he did.

Finally Gino raised his eyes to the unfortunate young man in front of him. "So, your man failed."

"Chaz was arrested."

"Why?"

"The window was connected to an alarm."

"You said your man could disarm an alarm."

"He did."

"What happened?"

"There was a backup."

Gino was not surprised. He hadn't actually expected Donnie's man to complete the mission.

Since succeeding his uncle as crime boss, he'd been trying to find Carlo's murderer. Recently he'd had a breakthrough while watching the Golden Globes, when **Desperation at Dawn** had won Best Dramatic Picture. Producer Billy Barnett had accepted the award. The name rang a bell. Gino remembered his uncle's troubles had started when a couple of his men had gotten arrested trying to abduct a producer's wife. The producer had been Billy Barnett.

Gino couldn't be sure if this Billy Barnett was just a coincidence or pay dirt. He'd sent Donnie's man as a test. It was a simple job. Break into the producer's house and kill him. If he did, Billy Barnett was innocent. But if Barnett lived, it would prove he was far more protected than a mere producer had any need to be.

Gino stared Donnie down. "So, your man didn't check for a backup system and got himself arrested. What did he tell the cops?"

"Nothing. He didn't talk, and we bailed him out."

"That either means he said nothing, or he spilled his guts."

"Chaz wouldn't do that."

"So you say. This man is a loose thread. Remove him."

6

Donnie Martel was in trouble. He'd realized he was the minute he set foot in Gino Patelli's office. He just hadn't realized how bad it would be.

Take out Chaz Bowen? Not a boss on Donnie Martel's level. He didn't have the resources. He didn't have the men. Chaz was the only hit man on his roster. Martel wasn't one of the big boys who ordered a hit every other week. He was pretty near the bottom of the totem pole, and it was never brought home to him more forcibly than at times like these.

The order had come straight from Gino Patelli's lips, which made it super important, something he had to put his best man on. Unfortunately, his best man was Chaz Bowen.

Donnie went back to his office, always a mistake coming straight from Gino Patelli's. The contrast was just too striking.

Donnie's office was in a section of downtown L.A. that looked like it was just about to be torn down and renovated. He parked on a side street, pushed the downstairs door open, and walked up the steps. His office was on the second floor over a sushi parlor. He'd been there so long he barely noticed the smell of fish.

Sophia was at the front desk reading a gossip magazine. Any other day he wouldn't have cared. Today it pissed him off.

"Don't you have work?" he snapped.

"Nothing pressing. I'm going to finish my coffee and tackle the bills."

Sophia was Donnie's entire office staff. She functioned as his secretary, receptionist, switchboard operator, typist, file clerk, and bookkeeper. She could also take dictation, but it never happened. He'd have her sit on his lap to do it, and then he'd forget what he wanted to say.

"Any calls?"

"Chaz Bowen. He sounded pissed."

"I'll bet. Hold my calls."

Sophia frowned. "You want me to put them on hold, or—"

"Tell them I'm out of the office."

Donnie pushed his way into his inner office and closed the door.

Donnie's desk was a mess of papers, none particularly important. He had a small protection racket on the south side, with half a dozen collectors and a couple of enforcers who were hardly ever needed. After the first visit, clients paid right up.

Donnie sat down at his desk and put his head in his hands. Half of his muscle wasn't as good as Chaz. The other half **was** Chaz.

Should he bring in someone from outside? Not likely. That was apt to cause more problems than it solved.

Donnie sighed heavily. He got up, lifted down a picture from the wall, and spun the dial of his safe. It had been a while, and he missed the combination the first time. He concentrated and got it on the second try.

Donnie opened the safe and took out a gun. It was an automatic with a full magazine and a round in the chamber. He took out a silencer and screwed it onto the barrel of the gun just to be sure. It fit.

Donnie locked the safe. He went over to the closet, pushed the coats and jackets aside, and found an old shoulder holster that hadn't been used in years. He used to wear it to impress people. After a while he realized it didn't make him look like a crime boss, just a low-level thug.

Donnie stuck the gun in the holster. The barrel was too long with the silencer. He unscrewed the silencer, and slipped it in his jacket pocket. He adjusted his jacket and tie and went out.

Chaz Bowen lived in the second-floor apartment of a brownstone in east L.A. Donnie deciphered his name from the scotch-taped name tags peeling away from the buzzers, and rang the bell. There was no answer. He rang it again. Finally the intercom clicked on and a groggy voice growled, "Who the hell is this?"

"Donnie Martel."

Moments later the door buzzed open. Donnie went up the steps to find Chaz hanging out his apartment door.

"You want to tell me what the hell happened?" Chaz demanded.

"I don't know what the hell happened," Donnie said, and walked in the door.

"You give me an assignment and you don't know what's going on? Piece of cake, you said. How hard can it be? Movie producer." Chaz snorted. "If that guy's a movie producer I'm a state senator."

"I'm just as surprised as you are. We're looking into it."

"'Looking into it'? Not good enough. I'm charged with attempted burglary. I can't afford a conviction. What are you going to do about that?"

"Just keep your mouth shut and you'll do fine."

"That's what the lawyer said. Then I got charged."

"And released. That's the important thing. Don't worry about the charge. It'll never get to trial. The important thing is you're out on bail. You keep quiet, we keep you out of prison, that's the deal. Let's drink to it. You got any booze?"

"I got some sour mash."

Donnie repressed a shudder. "Great. Pour me one."

Chaz went to the cabinet and took out the bottle of whiskey.

Donnie stepped up behind him and shot him in the head.

. . . .

Donnie was riding a huge wave of adrenaline. He got out of there fast, stopping only to wipe down any surface he might have touched. He skipped down the stairs, got in his car, and took off. Twenty blocks away his hands were still shaking.

Donnie pulled off by the side of the road, put the car in park, and tried to calm down. He'd done it, that was the main thing. Gino had backed him into a corner, and he'd managed to get out. There was nothing to connect him to the crime.

Except the gun. Small detail. He had to ditch the murder weapon. Where?

His first impulse was to throw it in the ocean, but he was in East L.A. How about a dumpster? The idea made him nervous. Should the gun be found, could it be traced back to him? No, he hadn't bought it in a store. But could it be traced back to the guy who sold it to him?

Donnie put the car into drive and took off. He was driving on autopilot, still playing it over in his mind. The bottle smashing on the floor. Jumping back from the spray of sour mash. Had he gotten any on his clothes? No matter. They were off to the cleaners in the morning.

The car, as if it had a mind of its own, had driven into the Santa Monica hills. He reached a curve in the road overlooking the bay. He stopped the car and got out; he walked to the edge of the bluff and looked down. He could see the waves lapping against the cliffs below. There was no one in sight. He took out the gun and unscrewed the silencer. He polished the gun with his handkerchief and hurled it over the edge. It splashed into the water.

Donnie heaved a huge sigh of relief and turned to go.

What about the silencer? Could they match the fatal bullet to the silencer it had been fired through? Donnie didn't think so. But he wasn't sure. That was a pain in the ass. Good silencers were expensive and hard to come by.

So was his peace of mind.

Donnie polished the silencer and threw it into the sea.

8

Teddy went down to the police station to find out about the status of his case.

The sergeant shook a gloomy head. "You'll have to talk to the ADA."

"Which one?"

"Rollins, I think."

ADA Jason Rollins wasn't any help. "We charged him, and he made bail."

"Charged him with what?"

"Attempted burglary."

"He was armed."

"Half the thugs we pick up are armed. They carry guns and don't take them off to commit a burglary.

It's not as if the judge made it easy on him. Bail was a hundred thousand."

"Who put it up?"

"The lawyer did. Good luck finding out who paid **him**."

"When will it go to court?"

The ADA shrugged. "Not for a few months. The case isn't even on the docket yet."

"So I can't find out what this creep was up to?"

"That's the way the system works. His rights are protected. Yours, not so much."

Teddy pulled up in front of Chaz Bowen's apartment building. It occurred to him he should have taken a production car. This was not the type of neighborhood in which he liked to leave his vintage Porsche. He went up on the front steps and checked the buzzers, finding the one marked Bowen, 2A, but he didn't ring it. He inserted a short piece of metal into the door lock and had it open in ten seconds.

Teddy went up the stairs to 2A. He didn't bother to knock. The guy hadn't knocked on his door. Fair is fair.

Teddy kicked the door in fast, leading with his gun.

The body of Chaz Bowen lay facedown in the middle of the floor. He'd been shot once in the back of the head.

A whiskey bottle lay shattered around him.

From the look of things, Chaz Bowen had been dead for several hours and the killer was long gone, but Teddy still made a sweep of the apartment to make sure he was alone.

A familiar red-and-blue flashing light cast a faint glow in the apartment.

Teddy rushed to the window. He flattened himself against the wall and peered out.

A police car had stopped out front and two uniformed cops were getting out.

Teddy didn't wait to see what they were up to. He slipped out the apartment door and took the stairs up.

The brownstone had four floors. There was a fifth flight up, leading to an access door to the roof. The door was securely fastened by a heavy-duty chain locked with an equally heavy-duty padlock. Teddy made quick work of it. He pulled the chain loose, wrenched the door open, and stepped out onto the roof.

The brownstone next door was only three stories high. What a waste of real estate, Teddy thought.

He went back to the stairwell. The chain that had been holding the door shut was pretty long.

Teddy unwound it and pulled it free. He took it up on the roof, letting the door close behind him.

At the edge of the roof was a standpipe about six inches high. Teddy had no idea what it was for, but it looked solid. He looped the end of the chain around it and locked it with the padlock. He dangled the chain over the side of the roof and tested it. It seemed sturdy enough. He lowered himself over the edge of the roof and climbed down.

The access door to the roof of the three-story brownstone was locked from the inside, but there was a fire escape on the back of the building. Teddy dropped down onto it.

Lights were on in the third-floor apartment, and Teddy could see movement through the window. He sprinted down the fire escape to the first floor, hung off the bottom, and dropped to the ground.

Teddy was in luck. The backyards of the buildings connected. He was able to creep along until he got to the alley. He hurried down it and peered out into the street.

Teddy had parked his car a block away out of habit. He hurried to it, climbed in, and started the motor.

In his rearview mirror he could see the red and blue lights flashing as he pulled away.

Early the next morning Teddy was awakened by a banging on the front door. He rolled over in bed and checked the security system. It was the police.

Teddy pushed the intercom and said, "Just a minute." He pulled on a bathrobe and stumbled downstairs.

Teddy opened the front door and said, "Did you find out anything?"

That took the officer aback. "Find out anything?"

"About the break-in."

"Only in a manner of speaking. The man who attempted the break-in was found dead in his apartment last night."

"Are you kidding me?"

"No, sir, that's a fact."

"So, you don't know why this guy targeted my house, and now we'll never find out?"

"That the least of our problems. We have a murder on our hands."

"That's got nothing to do with me."

"Well, sir, you do top the list of people who might want the victim dead."

Teddy groaned. "That doesn't even make any sense. The guy tried to rob me so I killed him? I certainly hope you have a better theory than that."

"We're just running down leads." The officer turned and pointed. "That is your Porsche Speedster parked over there, isn't it?"

"What about it?"

"The police responded to a call last night of a man breaking into the downstairs door of the building where the victim lived."

"Well, I hope they had more luck investigating that break-in than they did mine."

"A car matching the description of yours was seen parked in the neighborhood about the time the police got the call."

"Did they get the plate number?"

"I'm not at liberty to say."

"You are, actually. You just don't have it because

they didn't get it. This is Hollywood. You know how many vintage cars there are in this town? Maybe it's an affectation, but I don't care. I'm not out to impress anybody. I happen to like the car."

"Where were you at the time of the crime?"

"Well, I don't know when the crime was committed. What time are we talking about, Officer?"

"Around eleven last night."

"Oh. Then I know exactly where I was. I was watching the news. I wanted to see how they reported the Oscar nominations. Not to brag, but my picture happened to get several."

The officer grinned. "You got an Oscar nomination?"

"Yes, I did."

"What movie?"

"**Desperation at Dawn.**"

"Really? I loved that movie."

"You've made my day. That, Officer, is more important to me than an Oscar. It's nice to get good reviews, of course, but what you really want is a film that people enjoy. If you can do that, you're doing your job." Teddy smiled. "See, with all that happening yesterday, you can understand how I find it hard to relate if some punk gets whacked in his apartment. How was he killed, by the way?"

"Single shot to the head."

Teddy considered, nodded. "Cinematically good. You know how we do it in the movies with blanks and blood bags, but, of course, it's not the real thing. You'll keep me informed on how this turns out?"

10

Sylvester looked like someone out of a Charles Addams drawing, but the man had a sense of humor, be it somewhat macabre. "Are you interested in irony?"

Gino Patelli looked up from the racing form he was studying. He seemed annoyed at being interrupted. "I'm interested in results," he said. "You got any results?"

"Yes, I do. They just happen to be ironic."

"You mind spitting it out?"

"Not at all. The police have a suspect in the murder of Chaz Bowen."

"Oh, yeah? And who is that?"

"Billy Barnett."

"What?"

"A man of his description was seen breaking into the building, and his car was seen parked in the vicinity around the time of the crime."

"And when was that?"

"Eleven o'clock."

"Is that when Chaz was killed?"

"I think so. I'd rather not call and ask. I think the less contact we have with Donnie Martel the better."

"Have the police gotten onto him yet?"

"I don't think so. So far, the only evidence they've come up with points to Billy Barnett."

"And that's all they've got on him? Just a car parked in the neighborhood?"

"According to my source."

"That's not much evidence."

"No, it isn't."

Gino cocked his head. "It seems like they should have a little more."

11

Sylvester signed up for the Centurion Studios tour. He didn't want to, but it was the easiest way for him to get onto the lot. As a result he found himself with a bunch of tourists oohing and aahing over old sets where movies once had been filmed.

He snuck away as quickly as possible and found himself in the production wing of Centurion Studios. The office of Ben Bacchetti, the head of the studio, dominated the wing. The offices of the producers and directors radiated out from there.

Sylvester passed the office of Peter Barrington and came to the office of Billy Barnett.

Sylvester sighed. Under any other circumstances he would have pushed his way into the outer office and sweet-talked the secretary into giving him a chance to find something useful. Only this was a case where he didn't dare let his visit, however innocuous, be associated in any way with the result. As things were, he needed a place to hide out.

A bathroom was possible, but inconvenient. A storeroom would be better. He spotted what looked like the door to one at the end of the hall.

Sylvester's expertise with locks, though not up to Teddy's standard, was still pretty good. He had the door open in less than a minute. He slipped inside and was rewarded to find a low-use storage cabinet, not with papers and pencils and daily shooting schedules and the like, but instead with a number of canvas tarps, cots, and chairs, the type of equipment apt to be brought out on a particular day to fill a particular purpose.

Sylvester set up one of the cots. He switched his phone to vibrate and set it for nine o'clock. Then he lay down on the cot and went to sleep.

At 9:05 Sylvester pushed open the storage room door and slipped out into the hallway. The building was still in use, but most people had gone home. Lights were on in the corridors, but most of the offices were dark, including Billy Barnett's.

Sylvester took two metal strips from his pocket and picked the lock.

The lock on the inner office was no more difficult than the one on the outer. Sylvester slipped in and closed the door behind him. He took a penlight out of his pocket and switched it on.

At first glance there was nothing of interest. The desk was nearly bare. The outbox was empty. A couple of screenplays were stacked on the far corner of the desk, a good indication they were something the producer had been putting off reading.

Sylvester searched the office. He found a wall safe underneath a movie poster. Smiling, he set out to open it. A few minutes later he was no longer smiling. Well, that was interesting. Sylvester could get into most office safes with little trouble, but this one had him stymied. The lock was much more sophisticated than any movie producer could possibly need. What could he keep in it? A hush-hush screenplay?

Whatever it was, Sylvester wasn't getting a look at it. He replaced the poster and looked around the office.

All right. It didn't have to be important, it just had to be personal.

Sylvester went to the desk. He opened the top drawer and was greeted by a number of papers, none of them personal. The one on top was a receipt for a takeout delivery. Billy Barnett had had a sandwich delivered and signed for it with a credit card.

Perfect. Sylvester pocketed the receipt, closed up the office, and slipped out the door.

12

Sylvester checked out Chaz Bowen's apartment building from across the street. He'd never been there, but apartment 2A was most likely the street-side apartment on the second floor. It was dark, but lights were on in several of the other apartments.

It had been a long day. Sylvester wasn't waiting for everyone to go to bed. If the apartment was on the second floor, it wasn't like he'd have to go past any other apartment to get in.

Sylvester crossed the street and inspected the door lock. It was as flimsy as he'd expected. He quickly jimmied the door and went up to the second floor.

There was a crime scene seal pasted over the crack between the door and its frame. There was no way to get in without disturbing it. That didn't bother Sylvester. Disturbing it was part of the plan. Sylvester clicked open a razor-sharp gravity knife and slit the crime scene seal right down the crack. The result was perfect. It could be readily seen, but it looked like whoever had done it had been trying to conceal it.

Sylvester shone his penlight around the apartment. He could see the outline where the body had lain on the floor. Was there anything there worth examining? Not really.

Sylvester sat at the desk and pulled open the drawers. He pawed through the top drawer and came out with Chaz Bowen's checkbook. He flipped it open. The checks were in the bottom half, the ledger in the top. He thumbed through the listing of checks and deposits.

The last entry was a cash deposit of two thousand dollars. That figured. Chaz had been getting five thousand for the Billy Barnett hit, twenty-five hundred up front. Clearly he'd held on to five hundred dollars and deposited the rest.

There was no notation for the source of the deposit. Sylvester smiled. Excellent. That would be what Billy Barnett was looking for, and this would be the dead end he came to.

Sylvester creased the page, so the ledger naturally fell open to it. He stuck the checkbook back in the drawer, slightly askew so it stood out.

Okay, that's what the intruder was doing.

Here's what he dropped doing it.

Sylvester took the credit card receipt out of his pocket and crumpled it up. He dropped it on the floor by the chair, where it might have fallen out of the pocket of someone sitting at the desk.

Sylvester glanced around the apartment. Was there anything else he could do? No, the receipt was enough. Anything else would be overkill.

Sylvester worked his way to the door and slipped out. Moments later he was in his car, surveying his handiwork. So, the bait was in the trap. The police had only to find it.

He considered calling in an anonymous tip, but decided against it. There was no need. Chaz Bowen's apartment was on the second floor. Tenants on the higher floors would be passing by it on their way to work in the morning. One of them would notice the violated crime scene and phone it in.

Billy Barnett would have a lot of explaining to do.

13

Viveca Rothschild was riding the high. She had been excited about the Oscars before, but never like this. She'd always been the underdog, never the front-runner. It was nerve-racking, as if she had something to lose. The more real the possibility became, the more terrified she became that it would be snatched from her grasp. This tiny seed of doubt was the only thing that kept her from thoroughly enjoying her nomination.

"Popcorn, who needs popcorn?" Cheryl asked, emerging from the kitchen with a big bowl. "What's a movie without popcorn?"

"Television," Marcy Scott said, and everybody laughed. "We're watching television."

"Yes, but it's television about the movies. And if you don't have popcorn you're a grouch."

Viveca laughed. "No grouches, no grouches. Only positive energy. This is the year of happiness and goodwill." She gestured toward the television. "Even those assholes can't spoil it."

The assholes in question were Mickey and Marvin, two Los Angeles critics whose TV review show had been known to make or break movies.

Despite a reputation for being snarky, Mickey and Marvin had always had a soft spot for Viveca Rothschild. Reviews of her work had been favorable, if condescending. Viveca always felt they damned her with faint praise.

It was not all in her head. The other two times she'd been nominated, they'd treated her like a little girl lucky to have been seated at the grown-ups' table. Mickey Stillhorn's dismissal had particularly stung: "For her, the nomination **is** the award."

Not this year. Critics had practically gushed in describing her performance in **Paris Fling**. She was clearly one of the big girls now. She deserved to be there, and she deserved to win.

"Who wants a drink?" Cheryl said.

"I do," Bruce said, lunging to his feet and following Cheryl in the direction of the bar.

Viveca frowned. Bruce's doctors had recommended that he take it easy with alcohol. They had tried banning it entirely, but Bruce insisted he'd be better at moderation than abstinence. This had not, so far, proven to be true. Viveca stopped herself from jumping up and telling him to tone it down. No negative energy, she told herself. She nibbled on the popcorn, and sipped her gin and tonic.

The reviewers were working their way through the categories, as had the Oscar presenters. It was a long wait. The amount of popcorn thrown against the screen was increasing exponentially.

Finally they reached her category.

"And for Best Actress—" Mickey said.

"All right!"

"Finally!"

"Well, it's about time!"

Mickey went on, "—it's turning into an interesting year."

The statement was met with surprise.

"What?"

"Interesting, hell! It's a runaway!"

"That's right, Mickey," Marvin said. "The frontrunner in a race that's been all but conceded is, of course, Viveca Rothschild in **Paris Fling**."

"And what a performance! One that, I must admit, knocked this reviewer's socks off. She had always earned kudos for playing the naughty femme fatale, but who knew she could step into a Cyd Charisse role without missing a beat?"

"You say Cyd Charisse, I say Marilyn Monroe, in **How to Marry a Millionaire.** Who knew she had it in her?"

"I'll say. It's the kind of bold move that, if it works, it's great, and, if it doesn't, you're a laughingstock."

"Well, she's got my vote, just for having the guts to risk watching her career crash and burn."

"All that made her pretty much an Oscar lock."

There were huge cheers from all.

Mickey held up his finger. "But not so fast. Suddenly we've got a horse race here, and I didn't see it coming."

"I didn't, either, but that's what happened. Relative newcomer, Tessa Tweed, who took the Golden Globe for Best Actress in a Drama, deserves a second look."

"I agree. She didn't win just because she was in a separate category."

"No, she won it on her own merits. And for the first time, we have to weigh the merits of her performance against the merits of Viveca Rothschild's. It's not apples and oranges here. These are two fine actresses."

"While Viveca Rothschild is still the front-runner, she'd better look over her shoulder. Because someone is gaining fast."

"And that someone is relative newcomer Tessa Tweed."

14

Viveca said nothing on the limo ride home. Every time Bruce tried to talk to her she cut him off. That concerned him. Had he done something wrong?

"I didn't drink that much," he muttered.

To Viveca his words were just another annoyance. "What?" she snapped.

"I'm not drunk. I was moderate."

"Of course you were," Viveca said. She patted him on the arm without paying any attention.

When the limo pulled up in front of her house, she didn't wait for the driver or Bruce to help her out. She hopped out and sailed into the house, slamming the door behind her.

She went to the bar and poured herself a drink.

"Could I have one?" Bruce said, trailing in after her.

She ignored him, snatched up the phone, and dialed Manny Rosen, a gossip columnist she knew. Manny had a reputation for ferreting out seedy stories, even if he had to make them up himself. Manny had been a good friend ever since he had killed a story about her being high on the set of one of her movies. He had not done it out of the goodness of his heart. Viveca had found out how much Manny was being paid for the story, and paid him double to bury it.

"What's up?" Manny said.

"I need some publicity."

"That's a first, you coming to me for publicity."

"Yes, well, Oscar nominations are out."

"I know. Congratulations."

"Don't congratulate me yet. I'm just nominated."

"This year you're going to win."

"Don't say that."

"Why not?"

"Don't jinx me. There's such a thing as tempting fate."

"Well, we wouldn't want to do that, would we? Very well, my congratulations are withdrawn."

"Stop screwing around, Manny. Do you want this story or not?"

"What story?"

"The one I'm going to pay you for planting."

Manny groaned. "Please tell me your phone's not tapped. No one busted you for drugs and made you wear a wire?"

"Did you happen to watch **The Mickey and Marvin Show**?"

"I never watch them unless I have a tip."

"They did their Oscar predictions episode."

"I'm sure they predicted a win for you."

"They said it's a horse race between me and a newcomer named Tessa Tweed."

"I'm beginning to get the picture."

"I thought you would. Now, here's the thing. I need a story. But it can't come from you. No offense, but it needs to seem legit."

"Now, why would I find that offensive?" Manny said.

Manny called Josh Hargrove at the **Culver City Chronicle**. The **Chronicle** was one of those Hollywood papers that walked the fine line between newspaper and gossip rag.

"Josh? Manny. I've got a story for you."

"Oh, come on, Manny. Not again."

"Josh, I'm offended. Here I am, bringing you a story, and this is the thanks I get."

"Yeah, right," Josh said tonelessly.

A year ago, Josh had been caught at a motel with an underage girl. A cop connection of Manny's had tipped him to the story, and though Josh was never charged, even news of the arrest would be irreparably damaging to his career. So Manny had given his rival an option: exposure and total disgrace, or a cover-up, for a price. Josh had been dancing to his tune ever since.

"You know my philosophy, Josh. There's only room in the paper for so many stories. You print the ones I want, there isn't room for the ones you don't want."

"What's the story?"

"Tessa Tweed."

"The actress?"

"That's right. She just got nominated for an Oscar. Well, I've got some dirt on her that might interest you."

15

Ben Bacchetti was furious. He slammed the paper down on his desk and snatched up the phone. "Get me Josh Hargrove at the **Culver City Chronicle**."

Ben's secretary was startled. "Sir?"

"No, scratch that. Is Billy Barnett in yet?"

"I think so."

"Ask him to step in, will you?"

Teddy walked into the office to find Ben still fuming. "What's the matter?"

"Did you see the **Culver City Chronicle** this morning?"

Teddy smiled. "Gee, it's usually on the top of my reading pile, but—"

"There's a story by a hack named Josh Hargrove. He wrote that Tessa Tweed got nominated for a picture where she doesn't even say her own lines!"

"What?"

"This lowlife scum says Tessa was dubbed in the editing room by another actress."

Teddy waved it away. "Ignore it."

"How can I ignore it? It's a lie, blatant libel, and I won't stand for it. Every line Tessa says in the movie is her and her alone."

"Oh, don't make that mistake," Teddy said.

"What mistake?"

"Saying every line is hers. That just invites every sleazebag reporter in L.A. to go over the film with a fine-tooth comb. They'll find someplace in the soundtrack where her voice had to be enhanced because it was being covered over by the sound of a gunshot, for instance, and point to it as proof that Centurion lied in its statement to the press."

Ben exhaled an angry breath. "Damn it."

"Hey, we're big enough for people to take pot-shots at, and that's a **good** thing."

The intercom buzzed. "The police are here for Billy Barnett."

"Excellent," Teddy said. "Maybe they have news."

Teddy went out and met the police in the hallway.

"Gentlemen. Any progress?"

"That's not why we're here. The crime scene was broken into last night."

Teddy frowned. "That makes no sense."

"Why not?"

"You already inspected the crime scene. What could anyone possibly want that you haven't found?"

"We were hoping you could tell us."

"Oh, come on, gentlemen. Just because the man tried to break into my house doesn't mean I know the faintest thing about him. A petty thug tried to rob me. Aside from that, you know as much as I do."

The cop extended a plastic evidence bag. "Do you recognize this?"

Teddy looked. Inside was his credit card receipt for lunch.

"Sure, I recognize it. It's a credit card receipt for lunch. It's my credit card, and I signed for it."

"This receipt was found at the crime scene."

"Today?"

"That's right."

"After the crime scene was broken into?"

"Yes."

"Well, there you have it. Whoever broke into the crime scene left that receipt."

"Wouldn't you agree the most likely person is you?"

"Is it your contention that, eager to get a report on the murder, I broke into the crime scene and left my credit card receipt so that you guys would come and see me?"

"Don't be facetious."

"You find that absurd?"

"I certainly do."

"Please give me a reason my credit card receipt would be at an obviously violated crime scene."

"You dropped it looking for something."

"Looking for what? Something incriminating? Can you think of anything **more** incriminating than this credit card receipt? Wow, good thing that's gone, or I might have been in trouble."

"That's very clever, but it doesn't account for this receipt. Do you have any explanation?"

"Obviously whoever hired this guy to break into my house planted the receipt to make trouble for me. Are you making any progress finding out who that might be?"

"That is not the focus of our investigation."

"**Focus?** God, I hate that word. When the cops focus their investigation it means they have a fixed idea and they are ignoring everything else. I prefer words like **broadening the scope**. It tends to give one a fuller picture."

....

While Teddy was arguing with the cops, one of the officers slipped away to the men's room.

Officer Murphy was lucky he'd caught this detail. It had been a while since he'd had anything to pass along to Sylvester, and an informant was only as good as his latest tip.

This was something Sylvester would want to know.

Murphy took out his cell phone and made the call.

Sylvester stuck his head in the door of Gino's office. "The police are questioning Billy Barnett about the receipt."

Gino looked up from his desk. "When?"

"Right now. I just got a call from my guy."

"Billy Barnett's down at police headquarters?"

"No. The police went to the studio."

"They're there now?"

"As of five minutes ago. Murphy's there with 'em."

"You think they'll haul him in?"

"For a credit card receipt? I doubt it. I think they'll get his statement and leave it at that."

"Make sure they do. Call Murphy and tell him to let you know when they leave, and whether Billy Barnett stays behind."

"What if he does?"

"Send Marco."

16

Teddy came out the side door of Centurion Studios and headed for his car. He had his own parking space, one of the few perks of being a producer that he actually valued. When movies were filming at Centurion, parking spaces were at a premium, as a hundred-plus crew members flooded the lot. Only the producer, the director, and the head of the studio had their own personal spaces.

Teddy's Porsche Speedster gleamed in the afternoon sun. Climbing into the car always cheered him up, making him feel like a kid again and not just a man driving home from his job. Teddy slipped into the driver's seat, started the engine, and pulled out of the lot.

A black sedan, parked half a block down the street from the studio entrance, pulled out behind the Speedster and followed.

Teddy spotted him at once. The driver was good; he had pulled out casually and blended into traffic. The average driver wouldn't have noticed the tail at all. But a man who had spent twenty years at CIA intelligence, outfitting and training agents for missions, wasn't about to miss a trick. There were no second chances in the secret service, and no getting rusty. Your training wouldn't allow it. Alertness became routine. Routine became instinct.

Teddy's finely honed senses picked up the car in the rearview mirror and immediately began to classify it. Most behavior he would usually dismiss as ordinary. Not this time. The sedan was crowding the car in front of him too closely in case he had to speed around it, and hogging the crown of the road so no one could pass him, both behaviors were associated with a car on a tail. Teddy could tell this was the real deal.

Teddy hung a right at the next intersection and headed up into the hills. He lived on Mulholland Drive, but he had no intention of leading the black sedan into his own neighborhood. He had in mind someplace more remote.

The black sedan was clearly following him. The driver had made every turn and given up the pretense of keeping cars between them. As the roads became narrower and winding, the black sedan shortened the distance, and plastered himself right on Teddy's tail.

Teddy sighed. That was the problem with the vintage sports car. It was built for speed on the open road, but practically useless when you wanted to run some son of a bitch off the road.

As soon as he had the thought, the black sedan pulled alongside and began crowding him.

A hairpin turn was coming up. Teddy could easily be pushed over the edge.

In anticipation, the black sedan inched closer, nicking his fender.

The curve was rushing at them. There would be no room to turn.

Teddy downshifted and popped the clutch. The sports car, grinding in the lower gear, dropped back. Just before he fell behind the black car entirely, Teddy swung the wheel and clipped the tail end of the sedan with his fender. Then he was clear of it, and the black car vaulted ahead, fishtailing from the impact as the driver fought to steer back in the direction of the skid.

The sedan was going way too fast. The driver had anticipated pushing the sports car off the road, but with nothing to push against and his own back end out of control, the driver fought desperately to make the turn. He almost did, screeching in a wide arc before mounting the shoulder, jumping the guardrail, and cascading down the mountain in a fiery heap.

Gino Patelli was reading a racing form when Sylvester came in. "Any word from Marco?"

"No. But there's a news report of a one-car accident in Santa Monica."

"Fatality?"

"Driver's dead. Car went off a cliff. Supposedly burned to a crisp."

"Was it a Porsche?"

"No details yet. The rescue crew has to send somebody down to the wreck to bring up the body."

"Surely they can tell what type of car."

"Maybe they can, but they don't have to tell me. I got Paulie on the way there to find out."

Sylvester's cell phone rang. He pulled it out, clicked it on. "Yes?"

"Who's that?" Gino said.

"Uh-huh . . . Hang on." He cradled the phone

against his chest and raised his eyebrows. "It's Marco."

"On the phone?"

Sylvester shook his head. "No, that's Paulie on the phone. Marco's the guy in the car."

Peter smiled at Tessa. "You don't have to read."

"I like to read."

"You don't have to try out. You have the part."

Peter Barrington was holding auditions on the soundstage at Centurion Studios. Tessa Tweed was already cast in the lead role. Indeed, Peter had written it for her. The rest of the roles were wide open, so the casting call was a bit of a zoo, as every actor in Hollywood wanted to work with the hot, young Oscar-nominated director.

"Well, let me put it this way," Peter said. "Much as I like to hear you read my lines, today I barely have time for it."

"Some of the people you're auditioning have scenes with me. I can read with them."

"They can read with the production assistant, too. I'm not going to have you read with a hundred people. Though I'm happy to have your input on who should get callbacks."

Tessa grinned. "Isn't this fun?"

"You enjoy it as much as I do."

A production assistant hurried up with a stack of pictures and résumés. He set them on the table next to the director's chair. "Here's the first batch of Lolas."

Peter looked at the huge stack. "I thought Deirdre was going to weed them out." Peter's casting director handpicked the actors who would get to audition.

"She rejected hundreds. This is what's left."

"Success is fatal, Peter," Tessa said. "Everyone wants to be in your picture."

The outer door opened and Viveca Rothschild burst in, followed by her agent. "Peter Barrington. So nice to finally meet you. And, Tessa Tweed. I love your work."

Peter rose from his chair to meet her. "Miss Rothschild, this is an unexpected pleasure. How can I help you?"

"I came to read, of course! You are the hot young

director everyone's talking about. Oh, this is my agent, Warren. Don't mind him. He thinks if I land a part without him I won't need him anymore. Relax, sweetie, it's just like it's always been. I get the part and you make the deal."

"Oh, dear," Peter said. "This is terribly embarrassing. I don't know who you set this up with, but the part of Claire is already cast. Tessa is playing it. I'm sorry you came all the way down here, but I'm not going to read you for a part you can't have."

"I appreciate that. But surely you have another role I could read?"

"Only supporting roles. I don't have another part for an actress of your stature."

"Good supporting roles are hard to come by. Is there one I'd be right for?"

"We're auditioning the part of Lola, the main supporting role. Tessa plays a bank president who is being held hostage by a gang setting up a bank robbery. Lola is the kidnapper's girlfriend. She's scheming, manipulative, and the brains behind the outfit."

"That's right in my wheelhouse."

"You can read for it if you want to," Peter said. "In fact, I'd be delighted if you did." He stole a look at her agent. "But I need to be up front that this is a supporting role. It won't pay anywhere near what you've been getting."

"Warren is duly warned," Viveca said. "Okay, I understand. Let's give it a shot."

"Are you doing the trailer scene?" Tessa said.

"That's right."

"Great. I'll read with her."

Viveca was surprised. Stars didn't read roles they were already cast in for the sake of an audition.

Viveca and Tessa accepted the script pages from the production assistant and walked out on stage.

"Okay," Peter said. "To set the scene. Claire has been kidnapped and kept in the trailer over the weekend. Lola is priming her to help them rob the bank when it opens Monday morning. Lola is tough as nails and has been treating her harshly, but it's been a couple of days, and Stockholm syndrome is starting to set in. So, Viveca, you have a grudging respect for this woman, even though you hate everything she stands for."

The actresses started reading. In the beginning Peter followed along with his script. After the first few lines he put the pages down and just watched.

They were sensational. They played off each other perfectly, with a give-and-take that was subtle, nuanced, and right in character. For a cold reading, it was the best Peter had ever seen.

When they were finished, Peter said, "Oh, my God. Viveca, I don't know what to tell you. If I thought you would really take it, I would offer you this part right now. I would like nothing better than to have the two of you working together in this movie."

"So would I," Tessa said. "I don't know what that looked like out there, but it felt electric."

"Well," Viveca said, "I'm not hurting for money, but I am hurting for good, meaty roles. They don't come along that often. If you want to offer me the part, I want to take it. As for the rest, it can be negotiated."

Viveca turned to her agent. "Warren. Make it happen."

18

Viveca was pleased with herself. Crashing the audition had been a brilliant idea. She'd hoped to get the scoop about her competition, but she'd come away with something even better: a role with one of the hottest directors in Hollywood, and at a time when she'd had no new part on the horizon. She'd been picky since **Paris Fling**, not wanting to follow that triumph with a bad career move. It was tricky having pulled off a departure role. If she were to do another light musical comedy, it would be seen as a commercial move, just cashing in on her newfound success. Another comedy role would be nothing new, just a pale imitation of what she'd just done. She might even be offered **Paris Fling 2**, a complete sellout. A meaty character role was just what she needed. And she'd be playing opposite Tessa Tweed, a chance to show her up in a head-to-head competition. There were tricks to upstaging another actress, and Viveca knew them all. Tessa Tweed would never know what hit her.

Bruce was out in the home gym doing his exercises when she got back to her house. Viveca had outfitted the rec room just for him. Daily workouts were an important part of his regimen. Structured physical activity went a long way toward taking the edge off his post-traumatic stress. Barbells, floor mats, a chinning bar, punching bags (both speed and weight), a stationary bicycle, and an outdoor lap pool gave him all the physical activity he needed.

Bruce was cooling off with a moderate jog on the treadmill when Viveca came in. He slowed the machine, hopped off, and hugged her, not noticing how sweaty he was from the workout. It was the sort of social cue he was always missing.

"So, what happened?" he said. "Did it go well?"

Viveca extricated herself from his clutches. "It went very well. I got a job."

"What?"

"I got a part in the picture."

"In a Tessa Tweed picture?"

"Not her picture. Peter Barrington's picture. It's about a bank robbery."

"That's her picture. I saw her talking about it on TV."

"I'm sure you did."

"Will you be talking about it on TV?"

"I'm sure I will." Viveca exhaled. "You're sweaty. Go swim your laps."

"Okay."

Bruce went out the door and dove in.

Viveca went into the kitchen to make herself a drink. She was going to have a lemonade but decided on something stronger. She got out the blender and started whipping up a margarita.

It was amazing how Bruce could do that; send her crashing to Earth with some offhand comment. Yes, she'd be talking about it on TV. As would everybody else.

Damn.

She had taken a part in a film with Tessa Tweed. An excellent strategic move in terms of showing the public who was a better actress, but that wouldn't come until later, long after the Oscars. Right now the only public perception would be that she had taken a supporting role. **In a Tessa Tweed picture.** God, those words grated. Why did he have to phrase it that way? Unfortunately,

Bruce often put his finger on the simple truth. And that simple truth was what the immediate public reaction would be. Viveca Rothschild playing second fiddle to Tessa Tweed.

What an image to put in the minds of Oscar voters who had yet to cast their ballots. Would Academy members be influenced by the public perception? Of course they would. Academy members could be influenced if the wind changed. Otherwise she'd already have an Oscar.

This had to be handled with kid gloves.

Viveca went to the phone and called her publicist. "Annie, sweetheart. We've got to get out a release."

Annie laughed. "Don't we always."

"No, this is serious. I just signed on to do a picture."

"I heard."

"You heard?"

"That's why I'm the best publicist in Hollywood. I'm on top of things. That's what I do."

"We've got to get out a release, and it's important it resonate the right way with Oscar voters. The wrong publicity could cost me a win."

"Nothing's going to cost you a win, kid. I tell you, you're a lock."

"I signed on to do a picture with Peter Barrington

at Centurion Studios. We need to put out a release, and it must be before the studio does."

"Not going to happen."

"Why not?"

"The studio beat you to the punch."

"You're kidding."

"I'm reading their release now."

"Shit."

"Hey, I don't know what you're worried about. They did a perfectly adequate job. Not as good as I would, but all things considered."

"Damn."

"What's the matter?"

"We can't have Oscar voters getting the idea that Tessa is a star and I'm a supporting player."

"That's not the tenor of the release."

"'The tenor of the release'? Don't give me biz-speak. What does it say?"

"Nothing that's going to hurt you with Oscar voters. It says 'Oscar Nominees Tessa Tweed and Viveca Rothschild to Co-Star in New Film.'"

19

Teddy dropped the Porsche off at a body shop to get the front-end damage repaired.

The mechanic examined the crumpled fender and shook a gloomy head. "That ain't good."

"You should see the other guy," Teddy told him.

Teddy took a cab back to Centurion and found Peter in his office. "We have a problem."

"I'll say." Peter picked up a tabloid from his desk. "The gossip columnists won't quit. This one hints that the reason Tessa Tweed had all her lines dubbed was because she was drunk on camera and slurring her words."

"That's low."

"No kidding. Ben's ripshit, and it's all I can do to keep him from going after these guys."

"The worst thing he could do," Teddy said, "as I'm sure you told him."

"You bet I did. If I could keep him from reading the tabloids, I would."

"I'm afraid we've got more troubles than that."

"Oh?"

"Yesterday a car followed me from the studio and tried to run me off the road."

"Are you all right?"

"Aside from a dented fender."

"You think they'll try again?"

"He won't. I don't know who he worked for."

"You have no idea who's doing this?"

"No. I'm certainly going to make every effort to find out, but until I do Billy Barnett appears to be an endangered species. It occurs to me it might be a good time for him to go away on a location scout."

"I was actually going to propose it," Peter said.

"Oh? Why?"

"To make it easier for you to become Mark Weldon."

"Mark Weldon isn't in the picture."

Peter smiled. "He is now."

"What?"

"The public can't get enough of the man they love to hate. You got a Golden Globe and an Oscar nomination. It makes no sense not to have you in my movie. I intended for you to take a break on this one, so it didn't look like I'm working with a cadre of actors, what with Tessa already in it. But I realize that's just bad business. You have to give the people what they want, and they seem to want bad boy Mark Weldon. So I'm offering you the featured role of the bad guy. I certainly hope you take it."

"I don't know," Teddy said. "I'd hate to get a reputation for being typecast."

Peter blinked, then grinned. "You had me for a moment. So, that works. Billy Barnett goes on a location scout, and Mark Weldon shows up to rehearse. I take it you can arrange to delegate your responsibilities?"

"Hey, it's not my first rodeo. I'll be fine. But I must point out, Mark Weldon doesn't have a contract yet."

"It's all right," Peter said. "I don't pay Oscar nominees any less than other actors."

"You're all heart."

Teddy went down the hall to his office. His secretary was typing a letter.

"Margaret, I'm going on a trip to scout locations and will be out of reach, if anyone asks. You know the drill."

"How will I reach you?"

"I'll get you a cell phone number, and I'll check in from time to time."

Margaret was accustomed to Teddy's unorthodox style. She cocked her head and smiled. "You do know we're making a movie?"

Teddy grinned. "Thanks for reminding me."

20

Teddy went out to the long-term parking garage where he kept the Buick he used as stuntman Mark Weldon.

"I'm going to be gone for a while," Teddy told the garage man on duty. "Keep the space for me."

"As long as you keep paying for it."

Teddy took the car out. It looked exactly like what it was, a rough-and-ready secondhand jalopy, just good enough to get you there.

The car was filthy after months of disuse. Teddy drove it through a car wash on the way home.

Teddy pulled up his driveway and opened the middle door on the garage with the zapper in the glove compartment. He drove the car into the garage, locked it up, and went into the house, punching in the numbers to turn off the alarm.

Teddy got a suitcase out of storage, and brought it to his home office on the first floor. He pulled back the wooden double doors on the large closet, revealing the massive floor safe Mike Freeman had installed for him. Teddy didn't need to check if it had been tampered with. The slightest attempt would have triggered a dozen alarms. There weren't half a dozen people in the world who could have opened that safe.

Teddy was one of them. He was out of practice, so it might have taken him as much as ten minutes to pick the lock. Of course, he didn't have to. He had the combination.

Teddy swung the door open. Inside was a treasure trove of espionage equipment. He chose a handgun and shoulder holster; a sniper rifle, not the custom-made one he'd designed and handcrafted himself, but a perfectly serviceable CIA issue in a compact carrying case; a few burner phones, always useful; ten thousand in cash; and an assortment of credit cards, passports, credentials, and driver's licenses, along with the hair and makeup necessary to depict the men in the ID photos.

When he was done he locked the safe, went upstairs, and changed his appearance from producer Billy Barnett to stuntman Mark Weldon. He packed a few basic outfits to support his various identities, lugged the suitcase out to the car, and locked it in the trunk.

He backed out of the garage, zapping the door closed behind him. He pulled out of the driveway, keeping a sharp eye on the rearview mirror. No one seemed to be following him. He made a couple of figure eights just to be sure, then drove into town and parked around the corner from the apartment he'd rented in the name of Mark Weldon.

Paco Alvarez was out on the front stoop. As usual, the super wore a sleeveless T-shirt and was holding a beer in a paper bag.

His eyes lit up when he saw Teddy. "Hey, look who it is!" he said, saluting him with his beer. "Big-time movie star. I see you on TV, I say: Look who that is. You tell me you're a stuntman, like it's nothing, like you take any job you can get. Next thing I know you're on TV winning awards. So that's where you been, huh? That's why you can afford to keep your rent paid and not come around. You here for a while, now?"

"In and out," Teddy said.

He escaped from the super's clutches and lugged the suitcase up the stairs to his apartment. He unlocked the door, went in, and threw the suitcase on the bed.

Teddy wasn't happy. Mark Weldon's apartment was only useful as long as no one gave a damn about him. As just another stuntman he could come and go virtually unnoticed. He could pop into Mark Weldon's apartment, change his appearance, and pop out again; and if anyone noticed at all, they'd see just a small-time actor dressing up for a part. But as Oscar-nominated Mark Weldon, whose comings and goings would be trumpeted by a starstruck super and a brass band, he couldn't get out the door in another outfit without being asked what part he'd landed in what new movie.

Teddy had heard the phrase "success is fatal." He'd never really appreciated what it meant until now.

Teddy waited ten minutes, took the suitcase, and went back out the door.

The super was shocked to see him go. "Leaving so soon? I thought you were coming back."

"Just stopped by to pick up a few things. Like I said, I may be in and out for a while. We're gearing up to shoot a new movie."

"Really? What is it?"

"I can't really say until the studio announces it. I'll tell you when I can."

Teddy lugged the suitcase to the car, drove into downtown L.A., and checked into the Hyatt

Regency under the name Fredrick Sabbit, whose driver's license photo looked enough like Mark Weldon to get by the hotel clerk.

Teddy went up to his room and unpacked the clothes and hair and makeup items. He locked the IDs, cell phones, and cash in the hotel room safe. He locked the handgun and the sniper rifle in the suitcase, brought it back to the front desk, and asked them to put it in the hotel safe.

He went back up to his room, opened the safe, sorted through his credentials, and selected those of a Santa Monica police officer named Glen Hanson.

21

Teddy went down to the L.A. police station where a bunch of detectives were hanging out on their lunch hour. He took his shield out, flipped it open, and casually flipped it back. "Lieutenant Hanson, Santa Monica PD. Who can tell me the disposition of a B and E suspect, one Chaz Bowen, charged and out on bail?"

One of the detectives chuckled. "You're a little behind the times, Lieutenant. Chaz Bowen graduated to murder victim. He's got his own case file and everything."

"No shit. You got a suspect?"

"Nothing official."

"What does that mean?"

"No one's under arrest."

"And unofficially?"

"There's a guy looks good for it. Some movie producer."

"Oh, that can be messy."

"No kidding."

"Well, it makes my job academic, but I guess I gotta do it. When he was arraigned on the B and E, who bailed him out?"

"Damned if I know. You'd have to go over to the court."

"Oh, you don't wanna do that," another detective put in. "The court officer just loves giving cops a hard time."

"That's right. You're better off talking to Ruth."

"Who?"

Ruth was a property clerk at the police lockup who could have passed for the warden of a women's prison. Instead, she rode herd over items taken from arrested suspects and held until they were released. She also was the main source for all gossip relating to the department, including but not limited to the performance of their jobs and who was seeing whom on the side.

Ruth seemed insulted by Teddy's question. Why didn't he ask her a hard one? Who bailed out who was common knowledge.

"Ricky Fitz," she said promptly. "Mob lawyer. Handles a bunch of the players."

"Who'd you say?"

"Ricky Fitz. That's what everyone calls him. Name's Richard Fitzgerald. If he's involved, the client's connected."

"Connected to who?"

"Any number of small-time crime bosses."

"Which ones?"

Ruth shook her head. "I ain't naming names. That's how I got this job. Desk sergeant before me named names. Mobsters don't like being named."

The sign on the door read: SIMMONS, ATWATER, PROSKY & FITZGERALD.

Teddy went in and asked the secretary at the reception desk for Richard Fitzgerald.

"Do you have an appointment?"

"No, but he wants to see me."

"How do you know?"

"Because there are some clients he doesn't want to piss off."

The secretary blanched, got up from her desk, and disappeared into an inner office. She was back moments later.

"Mr. Fitzgerald may be able to see you. Could I have your name?"

"My name is not relevant to the current situation. My position is."

"What's your position?"

"I'm standing in his outer office with a gun in my shoulder holster."

The secretary blinked. "Follow me, please."

Teddy followed her into the inner office, where a rather slick-looking attorney sat behind a desk.

"Mr. Fitzgerald, this is the gentleman I told you about. He doesn't wish to give his name."

Fitzgerald waved him away. "I don't deal with anonymous clients."

"Do you deal with dead ones?"

"I beg your pardon?"

"You dealt with Chaz Bowen. He's your client. He's dead."

"What's that got to do with you?"

"You mind asking your secretary to step out? I hate to have witnesses."

"Is that a threat?"

"Don't be silly. We're just talking here. But attorney-client privilege does not apply in the presence of a third person."

"You want to hire me?"

"No."

Teddy stared him down. The attorney flushed and said, "That will be all" to his secretary. She was smiling slightly as she went out.

"Now then," Fitzgerald said. "What's this all about?"

"You like being attorney for the mob, don't you? Well, I have bad news for you. I'm not a cop. I'm under no legal obligation to show your clients the courtesy they deserve. I don't have to honor attorney-client privilege. I don't have to read people Miranda. So, this can go one of two ways. You tell me what I need to know, I leave your office, and no one will ever know that we had a conversation.

"Or, you can tell me to go to hell, and I'm going to go and get the information I need from another source. But I will be very careful to leave everyone with the impression that my sole source was you."

Teddy let that sink in for a moment. "So, when you find yourself with a contract on your head, you can console yourself with the fact that it's totally undeserved, and not the result of anything you did.

"Now then, start coming up with names."

Donnie Martel shot a thirty-seven on the back nine of Van Nuys. Never mind that he'd shot a forty-one on the front nine—he still had a round of seventy-eight, the first time he'd ever broken eighty on any course.

Donnie had a few drinks at the nineteenth hole, replaying the great shots in his mind, before driving home. He pulled into the underground garage, took the elevator up to his floor, and unlocked the door to his apartment.

There was a man sitting on the couch holding a gun.

Donnie blinked, uncomprehendingly.

He wouldn't have understood even if he'd been sober.

Teddy hadn't made himself up to be anyone in particular. His face didn't match any driver's license, passport, credential, or other ID. The only criteria had been that he not look anything like either Mark Weldon or Billy Barnett.

He'd also gone for mean. He wanted to be the scariest son of a bitch Donnie could ever imagine walking in on. Alcohol had dulled the effect somewhat; still, Teddy was thoroughly intimidating.

"Hi, Donnie," Teddy said. "I've got good news and bad news. You and I are going to have a little chat, and I'm going to ask you some questions.

"The good news is I'm not going to kill you if you don't tell me what I want to know."

Teddy flipped open a razor-sharp, stiletto-pointed gravity knife. His thin-lipped smile was positively chilling. "The bad news is you'll wish I had."

Gino Patelli. The name meant nothing to Teddy. So, a man he didn't know wanted him dead. Not an earth-shattering event for Teddy. He probably didn't know half the men who wanted him dead.

Teddy whipped out his cell phone and googled Gino Patelli, with surprisingly few results. Most references were recent, within the last few years. Without a Wikipedia page, it took a while to sort out why.

Gradually Teddy pieced together the information.

Gino Patelli was the ne'er-do-well playboy son of Vinnie Patelli, a low-level mob enforcer gunned down in an ancient turf war. Gino's mother, Rosa, had died in childbirth, so the death of his father left him orphaned. Rosa's brother, Carlo Gigante, took the boy in under his wing and taught him the family business. When Carlo wound up dead at the bottom of a cliff overlooking the ocean, Gino, having suddenly inherited his uncle's empire, stepped in and proceeded to rule it with an iron hand.

That all made sense to Teddy. While he had not killed Carlo Gigante, there was certainly reason to think that he had. Teddy had set into motion the events that led to his death; the fact that he did not actually commit the deed hardly absolved him from the responsibility.

The circumstantial evidence was compelling. Carlo Gigante had sent goons to kill Billy Barnett's wife. Teddy had accosted Carlo in an L.A. night-club, beat up his bodyguards, and threatened to kill him. Carlo Gigante had subsequently wound up dead. Gino Patelli would have no problem doing the math.

Teddy looked up Gino's address and drove out there. What he saw was not encouraging. A stone mansion like a giant fortress set back from the road behind an iron gate. A fence topped with barbed wire and no doubt electrified. Grounds protected by floodlights and probably dogs.

Teddy sighed.

He could kill Gino Patelli, but it would not be easy. It would require planning and execution. Above all, it would require time.

Teddy was about to shoot a feature film, a long and painstaking process, which required him to be somewhere else and to be someone else.

Mark Weldon was a bad guy in the movie, a stone-cold killer, but for all that he was a pussycat compared to Teddy Fay. Mark Weldon could not go on a killing spree in the middle of a movie shoot.

Teddy chuckled.

It was probably even in his contract.

23

Gino Patelli was frustrated. "Where the hell is he?"

"I don't know."

"Why don't you know?"

"I've got two men in separate cars staking out the studio," Sylvester said. "Barnett hasn't entered the lot since they've been on the job."

"But he's working there?"

"He's producing a movie."

"Then how can he not be there?"

"I have no idea. I tried calling his office and just got the runaround. He's supposedly on a location scout, but I can't find out where, what he's scouting, or when he'll be back. His secretary can't be pinned down, and is delightfully vague. Mr. Barnett can't be reached, can she take a message? Whatever I want to talk to him about, she'll take it down and pass it on the next time he calls in."

"Shit. But he's got a movie going now?"

"That's right. Gearing up to film."

"Then he's gotta be around. After the run-in with Marco, he must be taking precautions. He's found some way to get on and off the studio grounds without going through the main gate. He's there, but he's primed his secretary to say he isn't."

Sylvester nodded. "That could be."

Gino raised his finger. "We need someone inside."

Sylvester went down to the night court where the early-morning arrests were being processed. He waited through an endless string of drunks and hookers until he finally found what he wanted. A young man in his early twenties, groggy and disheveled from a night in jail but still handsome enough with curly dark hair and a pleasant face.

"Who do we have here?" the judge said.

"Dylan Foster," the prosecutor said. "Possession of a controlled substance."

Dylan had been arrested holding half a gram of cocaine. He pled nolo contendere and was sentenced to a fine of five hundred dollars or ten days in jail.

Dylan didn't have five hundred dollars, and was on his way back to the lockup when Sylvester stepped up and paid the fine.

Dylan was nervous, and rightfully so. He had no idea who this strange man was or why he'd bailed him out. He had half a mind not to go with him. But the prospect of sitting in jail for ten days tipped the scale. And the man was thin and cadaverous, didn't look that tough. Dylan figured he could always get away.

Dylan allowed himself to be led outside to a waiting car. The driver hopped out and opened the door to the back seat. Dylan glanced around, saw no way out, and climbed in. The thin man climbed in beside him. The driver got in and the car took off.

Dylan was afraid to ask where they were going. He wasn't sure he wanted to know the answer.

The car drove out of town and pulled into the gates of what turned out to be an imposing-looking mansion. The gaunt man ushered him up the steps and through the door.

Two burly men approached Dylan. The gaunt

man shook his head. "No need. He just came from lockup."

"Orders," one said. He took hold of Dylan and patted him down.

When the search found nothing, Dylan was marched down a wood-paneled hall.

They reached a door where another burly man patted him down, before stepping aside to let them in.

Gino Patelli looked up from his desk. "What have we got here?"

"This is Dylan. Found him in night court."

"Oh?"

"He's an 'aspiring actor,'" Sylvester said with mocking condescension. "Pled guilty to possession. I got him out for a five-hundred-dollar fine."

Gino looked the young man over critically. "You a junkie?"

"No, I did some lines at a party—"

"Don't care," Gino interrupted. He frowned, shook his head. "Kid's a wreck. Clean him up and he might do okay."

Dylan flinched.

Gino laughed. "Relax, kid. No one wants your body. Here's the deal, I'm going to get you a job on a movie lot. Not an acting job, probably production assistant, but a chance to make contacts, meet all the people you need to know. That something you'd like to do?"

Dylan paused. "What will you want in return?"

"Be my eyes and ears on the scene. You gotta see what I want to see, hear what I want to hear." Gino stopped, raised his finger right in Dylan's face. "There's only one thing you cannot do. You cannot leave. You cannot say, I've got a better gig, I'm moving on. You will not be moving on. If you try, you will be reminded of your obligation in rather dramatic fashion. Is that clear?"

"Yes, sir."

"Good. You're going to get a job at Centurion Studios. It's a big studio with lots of movies filming, and lots of producers. The only one I'm concerned with is Billy Barnett. I want you to report everything you find out about Billy Barnett. In particular, I want to know when he's on the lot, and what he's up to. You got that?"

"Yes, sir. And what do you want with Billy Barnett?"

"None of your fucking business."

24

Sylvester made some phone calls. Third time was the charm. The owner of an L.A. nightclub knew a guy who knew a guy who was a procurer of young girls for a movie star, and Sylvester was able to cut through the bullshit and pull in a favor. Two hours later he got a callback saying the way had been paved.

Sylvester called Hal Lindstrom, an assistant production manager at Centurion Studios, and said he had a young man who wanted a job.

Bright and early the next morning Dylan presented himself at the main gate.

"Dylan Foster to see Hal Lindstrom."

The guard consulted a clipboard and nodded. "Go right ahead."

"Where will I find him?"

"In the production office."

"Where's that?"

"Go in the front door and ask anyone."

Hal Lindstrom turned out to be an older gentleman, bald, with wispy white hair over his ears. "Dylan Foster, eh. They told me you'd be coming in. So, you want to be a production assistant?"

"I really want to be an actor."

"Of course you do. But that's not what today is all about. I need production assistants willing to do the job because it's long, hard hours, and you don't get overtime. If you think you're just going to hang out with the actors all day, you won't last. You're going to be a gofer. You know what that is? Someone wants something, you gofer it. You got a driver's license?"

"Yes."

"Good. You'll be running errands for all departments. Everyone's your boss, but it gets filtered through me. Costume department wants you to pick up some cloth, you say, Gotta run it through Hal. That way I know where you are and what you're doing and you won't get assigned two things at once. You got a cell phone?"

"Yes."

"Good. Give me a call. Your number goes on my contact list, so I can call you if I need to. Often I'll have something else for you to do, and it won't pay for you to come back here first. Got it?"

"Yes, sir. When will we be on the set?"

Hal made a face. "See, that's the trouble with PAs. Starstruck. Filming's just one part of the job. We've got four pictures filming right now, but you ain't going on them. Unless it's an emergency, we don't hire someone and throw them onto an active set in the middle of the shoot. We got a film that just finished casting going into rehearsals. That's where you'll start."

"What film?"

"**Trial by Fire**. It's a Peter Barrington film. He's the writer and director."

Dylan controlled his reaction. Billy Barnett was Peter Barrington's producer. This task might be far easier than he'd anticipated.

A young man about Dylan's age came into the office. He had red hair, glasses, and a somewhat gooney grin.

"Sandy. This is Dylan. He's starting today, first day as a gofer. Take him around, show him the ropes."

"Sure thing."

"What are you up to, Sandy?"

"Taking out a production car. I need to pick up toilet paper for the actor's trailer."

"Take Dylan with you. You go with Sandy. He's been with us a while, knows the business. Production assistant is a very important part of the film crew."

"Yes, sir," Dylan said.

"Come on," Sandy said, waving his arm. "Let's hit the road."

25

Dylan lugged a case of beer out of the convenience store and loaded it into the trunk of the production car.

"You gotta be shitting me," he said, as Sandy pulled the car away from the curb.

"What do you mean?"

"Is that all it is? Our glamorous life in the movies? All beer and toilet paper?"

"Hey," Sandy said, "a famous actress will be using the toilet paper. A famous actor will be drinking that beer."

"I doubt if they'll be drinking it with me. When do we meet these people?"

"Relax. You're just like everyone else who starts off in the movies. Where's the glamour? Where's the glitter? Where's the prestige?"

"Well, I'm sure it's not all like this," Dylan said. "I could be a grocery store delivery boy and probably make more money."

Sandy smiled. "You are free to quit."

"Hey, now. Don't rat me out to the boss. I'd like to last longer than a day."

"Don't worry, you will. Unless you walk off."

"I'm not going to walk off. But when do we have fun?"

Sandy grinned. "This is the fun."

"What are you talking about?"

Sandy pointed at the dashboard. "Driving around in a brand-new convertible with the top down and a sign for CENTURION STUDIOS on the dash. If you want to impress the girls, this is the way to do it."

Sandy didn't really look like the type to get a girl's heart racing, but Dylan let it go.

Sandy drove back to Centurion. The guard waved them through the main gate.

"They don't check your ID?" Dylan said.

"They know me, and they know the car. Production car with a Centurion logo goes right in."

Good to know, Dylan thought.

They dropped the toilet paper off at the

maintenance closet, and put the beer in the cooler in the cafeteria kitchen.

"What now?" Dylan said.

"We report to the production office to see what Hal wants us to do."

"If he had anything he was going to call. He must not have anything."

"What's your point?"

"No one wants us just now. Don't you want to show me the layout?"

Sandy considered. "All right," he said. "You've been a good boy. I'll give you a treat."

26

Peter held up his right hand and stopped the rehearsal. "Mark, rein it in some."

Teddy frowned. "I'm overacting?"

"You're fine," Peter said. "But we've got Viveca now, playing your henchman. If we're getting the same thing from both of you, it's one-note. I need the contrast. If you pull your character back and make him slightly reasonable, she can be the one that's going too far."

"You want me to play that?"

"What?"

"That she's exceeding my authority, and it annoys me?"

"Yes." Peter nodded his head. "Play that. Tessa,

same from you. Viveca is the true threat, so Mark is virtually the voice of reason."

"Despite the fact he's kidnapped me and is threatening to abduct my son," Tessa said ironically.

"Exactly."

Tessa grinned. "I like it."

"Does that work for you, Viveca?"

Viveca cocked her head. "You want me to be a crazy bitch?"

"Well," Peter said, "I don't want to hurt your image, but—"

Viveca laughed. "Just yanking your chain. I love it. You want a crazy bitch, you got her."

"Excellent," Peter said. "Don't be surprised if I make some slight changes in the script to reflect those attitudes."

Peter was rehearsing on soundstage four with Teddy, Viveca, and Tessa. In the film, Tessa is abducted, thrown in the trunk of a car, and held captive in a trailer park while the robbers set up a bank heist. Tessa plays a bank president who's being coerced into taking part in their plan. In the scene, Teddy and Viveca are programming her for what she has to do. For the purpose of the early rehearsal, aside from Peter, only Francine, the script supervisor, was on hand taking down notes.

Sandy and Dylan came in. They had been

listening at the door during the scene, and only entered while notes were being given.

Peter looked around. "Hi, Sandy. You need something?"

Sandy put up his hand apologetically. "Don't want to interrupt. I just wanted to let you know we have a new production assistant. This is Dylan. Anything you need, if I'm not around, he's your man. Dylan, this is Peter Barrington, the director. Anything he wants trumps anything anybody else wants."

"Pleased to meet you," Peter said, shaking Dylan's hand. He indicated the actors. "You probably recognize these guys. Mark Weldon, Viveca Rothschild, and Tessa Tweed. You may wind up doing things for them, too. But watch out for Mark. If he wants you to kill someone, check with me first."

Dylan came out of the soundstage with a big grin on his face. "Now that's a little more like it!"

"See?" Sandy said. "It's not all beer and toilet paper. Are those girls hot, or what?"

"Girls?" Dylan said. "That's Viveca fucking Rothschild! The Blonde Bombshell! Good thing I didn't have to say anything, or I'd have been tripping all over my tongue."

"You get used to it," Sandy said. "By the end of the week she'll be just another person who wants something done."

"I don't think so," Dylan said. "So that's the director. Who's the producer?"

"Billy Barnett. He does most of Peter's movies."

"Is he around?"

"Haven't seen him. He'll be on the set once we start shooting. He's the type of producer who shows up, jokes with the crew, and gets things done."

"Doesn't he help with the casting?"

"We're all cast. Locations are all pinned down. We've got a start date and a shooting schedule. Trust me, we're a well-oiled machine."

"Sounds like we've got nothing to do. Do we get the rest of the day off?"

"As if." Sandy checked his watch. "We have a little time. You want to stroll around, familiarize yourself with the place, meet me in the production office in a half an hour?"

"Will do."

Dylan wandered around the studio, trying to look like he belonged there. He felt funny about it, since as a legitimate employee he **did** belong there.

It was his secret mission that made him feel like an interloper.

He walked past the office of Ben Bacchetti, the head of the studio and Tessa Tweed's husband. It was good he knew that. Tessa Tweed was young and beautiful, but taken. He'd keep his distance.

Viveca Rothschild, on the other hand . . .

Dylan smiled and walked down the hall.

He passed by Peter Barrington's office. Peter was on the soundstage, but it was good to know where to look for him when he wasn't. A thought crossed Dylan's mind: Could he hit him up for a part? No one said he couldn't. As long as he got his job done, what could it hurt?

The sign on the next door said BILLY BARNETT. Dylan took a breath and pushed his way in.

A woman was typing at a desk. She looked up when he came in.

"May I help you?"

"This is Billy Barnett's office?"

"It's his outer office. I'm Margaret, his secretary."

"Pleased to meet you. I'm Dylan. I was just hired as a production assistant for Mr. Barrington's movie. Mr. Barnett's producing it, so I thought I should introduce myself. He is producing it, isn't he? I'd hate to get everything wrong my first day."

"Oh, he's producing it, all right. He isn't in today, but I'm sure you'll run into him on the set. He's a very busy man, always in and out. But don't let that intimidate you, he's really very nice."

Dylan smiled and went out. He figured that was too bad, but it was too much to hope for, fulfilling his job on the first day. Then he'd be done with these penny-ante gangsters, and he'd still have a job in the motion-picture industry, the kind of job you couldn't get without connections. It was perfect. If he could just get rid of his connections, he was all set.

27

Sandy took Dylan out to a bar where the production assistants hung out after work. It was a beer-and-buffalo-wings type of place, and reminded Dylan of college.

Sandy introduced Dylan around. All the production assistants seemed obsessed with movies. One of them, Roger, knew more than most, or at least he acted like he did. Dylan took an instant dislike to Roger, who was insolent and condescending. He struck Dylan as one of those people who equate bad manners with genius.

The only other PA who stood out was a college-aged girl named Stacy. She was not beautiful in a movie-star way, but she was cute, with a button nose and a ponytail. She took an instant shine to Dylan, which would have been nice, but he saw immediately that it seemed to upset Sandy. Sandy clearly had feelings for her, and she just as clearly didn't return them. The fact that she was interested in Dylan was an unfortunate complication he simply didn't have time for, not with a bunch of goons expecting him to function as a secret agent.

Dylan sipped his beer and wondered how he was going to handle the situation.

Roger wouldn't let up on him. "So, you want to get into production, do you?"

"Actually," Dylan said, "I want to be an actor."

"Oh, there's a shock," Roger said, and everybody laughed. "Everyone wants to be an actor. One of the first things you have to come to terms with when you start work here is you're not going to be an actor. Resign yourself to that and you'll get along fine."

"Have you resigned yourself to that?"

"Oh, I **am** going to be an actor," Roger said, and everyone laughed again. "I was talking about you. New kid, don't know shit, haven't had your dreams pounded out of you yet."

"Hey, don't sugarcoat it," Sandy said, wryly. "Let the kid know what he's in for."

"Why couldn't he make it?" Stacy said. "Nobody's seen him yet."

Roger scowled at being cut off in mid-flow. "What the hell does that mean?"

Sandy leapt to her defense. "Hey, take it easy, Roger."

Stacy didn't need help. She stuck to her guns. "We've all been around for a while. Anyone who could help us already knows us. If anyone was going to make one of us a star, they've had ample time to do it. But Dylan's new. Maybe someone will see something in him they like."

Dylan found the conversation uncomfortable on so many levels. He grinned, trying to diffuse the situation. "Hey, I know it's a pipe dream. I'm a starstruck kid. I can't wait till they start shooting."

"If you're around," Roger said.

For the first time, Dylan lost his cool. His face darkened. "Are you saying I'll be fired?"

"Relax. No one gets fired. You'd have to get drunk and crash a picture car the day before shooting."

"Picture car?"

"A car that's seen on-screen." Roger cocked his head. "You really don't know anything, do you?"

"Even so, don't expect to be on the set," Sandy said. "You're just as likely to be in the studio."

"Aren't we shooting in the studio?" Dylan said.

"And the kid swings and misses. Strike two," Roger said, and everyone laughed. "Sorry," he said. He didn't sound sorry. "But it's rare for someone to demonstrate such a profound lack of knowledge. Movies never start shooting in the studio. You shoot the exteriors first, all the location shots. Why? So if it rains, you can move indoors to a cover set. That's usually in the studio. If you shoot all the studio scenes first, when it rains you have no cover set as a contingency."

"So where will we shoot?" Dylan said.

Roger was in full lecture mode. "The two main locations in this film are a bank and a trailer park. The interior of the trailer's being built on the sound-stage. The bank we're shooting at is a bank. We've got other exterior scenes—-the abduction, the car chase, the kid in school. Barring rain, we won't see the inside of the studio for two weeks."

"You've seen the shooting schedule?" Dylan asked.

"It's posted outside the production office. You can only miss it if you're daydreaming about being a movie star when you walk by. Anyway, the first day's in downtown L.A. in the street outside the bank. Those of us that are working the set, that is." Roger smirked. "Don't expect to be."

That was the last thing Dylan wanted to hear. He didn't just want to be on the set.

He had to be.

28

Teddy had no one to be other than Mark Weldon that night, so he elected to stay at Mark's apartment just to keep up the illusion that he was living there. He even gave the super a thrill, sitting out on the stoop with him drinking beer and telling Hollywood war stories, only some of which were apocryphal.

"How'd you make your break?" Paco Alvarez wanted to know. "You're working as a stuntman, suddenly you're winning awards. That doesn't happen. It's like winning the lottery, am I right?"

"Exactly right," Teddy said. "Just being in the right place at the right time."

"And having talent."

"Everybody's got talent or they wouldn't be there. Getting a chance to show it is something else."

"So what happened?"

"I'm working as a stunt double for a well-known character actor. I'm not going to say which one, for reasons that will be obvious. The guy was one of those actors everyone loves, whatever he's in. So the director's delighted to get him in this part.

"Only the guy's a fall-down drunk. He goes off the wagon the night before shooting and gets in a bar fight, and the studio has to pull strings just to keep him out of jail. They manage to hush it up, but the guy's a mess. He's so hungover he can hardly stand. He's lost a tooth, and one eye's swollen shut.

"They've got me in costume ready to step in for the stunt sequence, so they just roll the scene and shoot me, figuring some of the footage will be usable if it's from an angle where you can't see my face. But they watched the footage they shot, liked it, and decided it made more sense to go on shooting without a drunk pain in the ass. Which they do, only his agent threatens to sue and they wind up paying his salary anyway. So the guy winds up making a hundred times what I do for **not** playing the part."

"Son of a bitch," the super said. He laughed heartily and pounded Teddy on the back. "Son of a bitch!"

Teddy finally escaped the super's clutches. He went to bed a little tipsy, and resolved never to get caught on the front stoop again.

29

Teddy's cell phone vibrated mid-rehearsal. He finished the scene and let Peter get through his notes before requesting a bathroom break.

He went out in the hall, pulled out his phone, and saw his secretary had called. Teddy ducked into his dressing room, closed the door, and called her back. "Hi, Margaret, what's up?"

"You have a meeting you didn't tell me about."

"Oh?"

"I cleared your schedule of everything on it, but Philip Manheim just called to confirm that you were still on for your luncheon at one o'clock at the Polo Lounge?"

"Oh, hell," Teddy said. "That's my fault. He

caught me in the middle of something else and I said yes and then forgot about it."

"That's what I figured," Margaret said. "Any particular excuse you'd like me to use when I cancel?"

"Like I got hit by a truck?"

"That would work."

"He'll just want to reschedule. Look, tell him I'm really sorry but I'm tied up at the studio and can't get away, and would it be a terrible imposition for him to meet me here for lunch?"

"At the same time?"

"Yeah, the same time. Actually, this will be a good barometer of his interest. If he's willing to pass up the Polo Lounge for cafeteria food, it's a pretty good indication he's serious about the project."

"Will do."

Things worked out well for Teddy. Philip was happy to come to the studio, and Peter was working with Viveca and Tessa before lunch, so Teddy was able to get away and become Billy Barnett.

No one was looking when he went down the corridor and ducked into Billy Barnett's office.

Margaret's face lit up in a smile. "Why, Mark Weldon. Delighted to see you." Her eyes twinkled.

"Would it surprise you very much to find that Mr. Barnett is not in?"

"He will be in a minute," Teddy said. "He's gotta get ready for this damn lunch. When Philip shows up, stall him."

Teddy went into his inner office and closed the door. He went to his closet and selected a suit, tie, belt, shoes, and socks.

He took his keys out of his pocket and unlocked the reinforced closet in which he kept a few special items, including a complete makeup kit. Then he went in the bathroom and transformed his appearance from Mark Weldon to Billy Barnett.

He hung up Mark Weldon's slacks and T-shirt, put the makeup kit back, and locked the closet.

He came out the door to find Margaret talking to a young corporate type.

Teddy smiled warmly, shaking his hand. "Philip. Thanks for helping me out."

30

Dylan dropped so many hints about wanting to be on the shooting set that Hal finally called him on it.

"Look, kid, I get it. That's where the glamour is. But these things go by merit and seniority. You haven't been around long enough to merit anything, and what does that say for your seniority? If I can get you on the set, I will, but don't count on it. Meanwhile, I don't want to hear about it. I got other things to do with my life."

Dylan knocked off for lunch feeling discouraged. Nothing was going his way. He'd spent the whole morning running errands, never got near the set, and he had no idea what was really going on at Centurion Studios.

Hanging over his head was the fact that this might not be conducive to his health. Gino Patelli's goons were apt to pull him in and squeeze him again, just for the pleasure of hearing his bones break.

Dylan wandered down to the cafeteria. Stacy was in line, holding a tray. She waved him over.

"You want me to cut the line?"

"It's not cutting the line if we're together. Grab a tray."

Dylan grabbed a tray and got in line just in time to see Sandy come in and give him the evil eye.

Stacy and Dylan got their food and sat down while Sandy was still in line.

"You know that Sandy has a thing for you?"

"Oh, for goodness' sake, he's not serious. He's like a dog trying to catch a car. He wouldn't know what to do with it if he did."

"That's cynical."

"I don't mean to be. Sandy's nice, he's just not my type."

"You have a type?"

"Are you flirting with me?"

"Sandy's a friend."

Stacy made a face. "Oh, my God. Am I back in high school? Slip me a note during study hall?"

"No, nothing like that," Dylan said. He stood up and waved Sandy over.

"What are you doing?" Stacy said.

"Well, I'm not sitting alone with you while my buddy has a fit," Dylan said.

He started to sit down and his face froze.

There, not three tables away, was Billy Barnett.

Stacy frowned. "Hey, what's with you?"

Sandy walked up with his tray.

"Hey, Sandy," Dylan said. "Is that Billy Barnett?"

Sandy looked before sitting down next to Stacy. "Yeah, that's him. I told you he'd show up."

Waiting a beat, Dylan put on a curious expression and pulled out his cell phone, as if it had pinged. "Sorry, guys, I have to make a call, family stuff. Hang on, I'll be right back."

Dylan slipped out of the cafeteria, dialing Sylvester as he went. He had him on speed dial. He hoped to be able to delete his number soon.

"It's Dylan."

"What's up?"

"Billy Barnett's here."

"Where?"

"At Centurion. He's in the cafeteria having lunch."

"Where are you?"

"In the hall. I slipped out to make the call."

"Get back in there. Don't let him out of your

sight. If he makes a move to leave, you go with him. And let me know the minute he does. This is pay dirt. Don't blow it."

Sylvester hung up the phone and called Frankie, one of the men staking out Centurion. "You see Billy Barnett?"

"No."

"He's there."

"He can't be."

"Well, he is. If he comes out, you better see him or you'll be looking for a new job. Tell Sammy. I don't want to have to make this call twice."

Sylvester slipped the phone back in his pocket and pushed his way into Gino's office. "He's there."

"Billy Barnett?"

"At Centurion, in the cafeteria having lunch. No one saw him go in, but he's there. The kid just called. He's watching him. I told him to call us if Barnett goes anywhere."

"You got men on the place?"

"Frankie and Sammy."

"Send Max."

"Two men aren't enough?"

"They didn't even see him go in! Call Frankie and Sammy back. If they didn't see him go through the main gate, there must be another way in. When Max gets there, have them fan out and find it."

"I'm on it."

"We should get a man in there."

"We got one."

"A man with a gun, for Christ's sake."

"You want me to give the kid a gun? No way that ends well."

"I don't care if he gets killed as long as he takes out Barnett."

"If he gets killed, fine. But what if he gets arrested? He knows who we are and he'll talk. Relax. We've got him spotted, and we'll know when he leaves."

"We **better** know when he leaves. Send Max and put the fear of God in them. I'm tired of this shit."

31

Frankie's car was across the street and down the block from the main entrance to Centurion Studios.

Max pulled up alongside and rolled down the window. "Where's Sammy?"

"Went to look for another entrance."

"You just thought of that now?"

"Guy's a fucking producer. Who'd expect him to sneak in a back entrance?"

"You can't expect him to do anything. You gotta plan for if he does."

Frankie rolled his eyes. "Hey, do I come around when you're working and bust your chops?"

"It ain't me. I hear Gino's having a fit."

"So help us out, willya?"

"That's why I'm here. Which way did Sammy go?"

Frankie pointed. "Around that way."

"Then I'll go around the other way and see what he missed. You sit tight. See how many actresses you can spot."

Max went around the back of Centurion Studios. He came to a gate leading to a loading dock. There was no one around to open it, but a big-shot producer might have a key.

Max found another locked gate behind the soundstages where scenery could be loaded in and set up. He found another gate behind which a fleet of trucks was parked, another gate that led to a scene shop, and yet another gate that a car across the road seemed to be staking out.

Max was not surprised to find Sammy in the driver's seat. "What're you doing?"

"They told me to find another entrance. I found it."

"You're staking it out."

"I don't want to get in trouble."

"That's the gate to the dumpsters. You think this producer's going to throw out his garbage?"

Sammy said nothing, just glared at Max.

"I assume this is the first gate you came to since this is the place you stopped."

"I didn't see anything else."

"I'm not surprised."

Max pulled off on the side of the road and called Sylvester. "There's half a dozen ways Barnett could have gotten in. None of them are likely. There's no back entrance for personnel, and there's not another manned gate. If the guy was intent on sneaking out through the kitchen or the scene shop or the delivery bay, it would mean getting through a locked, unmanned gate, but I would assume a producer could manage that. So, either you throw a lot more men on this place, or you have someone on the inside tip us off on which way he's going."

Sylvester hung up and called Dylan.

It went to voicemail.

32

Dylan got another cup of coffee and went back to his table and sat down.

Billy Barnett was still there talking to a man who looked like money, a somewhat plump man in a bespoke suit. They were also having coffee, which probably meant they'd be getting up soon. Dylan found his palms sweating.

Sandy and Stacy were just finishing up and getting ready to go.

"Aren't you coming?" Stacy said.

"In a minute, I just want to get another coffee."

"Hey, it's the movies," Sandy said. "When you need another coffee, you grab it to go."

"I'll be along."

After what seemed like forever, Sandy and Stacy bused their trays and went out.

Dylan heaved a sigh of relief. Billy Barnett and his companion were still there. If he'd chosen that time to leave, things might have gotten messy.

They did.

"There you are," a young woman said, swooping down on the table. Dylan recognized her as Francine, the script supervisor who sat in on Peter's rehearsals.

"Dylan, was it?" Francine said. "Just the one I was looking for. Dylan, you look to me like a Harvard man."

Dylan frowned. "What?"

She smiled. "I assume you can read. I've got a doctor's appointment. The actors are trying it off book this afternoon, and they need a prompter. Peter wants you."

"Really?" Dylan said. "But I'm the new guy."

"Yeah, you lucked out, kid."

"I know, but I don't want to step on anybody's toes. I mean, like, Sandy, you know?"

"Sandy reads like a truck driver." Francine made a face and glanced around. She relaxed. "Dodged a bullet. It would be just my luck to have a teamster sitting there. Anyway, Peter wants you, and he needs you now. Come on, let's go."

"Can I finish my coffee?"

Francine stared at him. "Are you stupid or what? When the director wants something, you jump. Get going."

Dylan glanced helplessly at the table where Billy Barnett was having lunch, and trotted off after Francine.

Rehearsal was wonderful. At least it would have been, if Billy Barnett had been there. Instead, Dylan got treated to the sight of two terrific actresses playing a scene. They knew their lines for the most part, and when they didn't Dylan was able to cue them with intelligence and inflection, two key qualities for a prompter so many people lacked. Dylan was making a good impression on the director, and he'd have been high as a kite if it weren't for the fact he knew he was in deep trouble with the mob, not the sort of thing that was apt to be conducive to his health.

Just when he thought the rehearsal was winding down, and it looked like they might take a break, Mark Weldon showed up, and Peter worked a scene with the three of them.

Dylan felt like his head was coming off. What the hell could he do? Billy Barnett wasn't going to stay at lunch forever.

33

Francine was back in an hour and a half. She breezed in during a break in rehearsal and said, "Miss me?"

"I didn't notice you were gone," Viveca said cheerfully. "I'd look out if I were you. I think Dylan's hot for your job."

Dylan flushed at hearing Viveca call him by name.

"Don't embarrass the kid," Francine said. "It's practically his first day. You wanna stick around and see how it's done, Dylan?"

Dylan's head was coming off. Was he ever going to get off the soundstage?

"I would, but I have work. Could I watch another time, Mr. Barrington?"

"Only if you call me Peter. Thanks for filling in. If Hal wants to know where you've been, use my name."

Dylan beat a hasty retreat.

There was no way Billy Barnett was still at lunch, but Dylan poked his head in the door. Of course, the cafeteria was empty.

Dylan hurried down the hall to Billy Barnett's office. Barnett's secretary was at the desk.

Dylan smiled, fighting the adrenaline, and tried to appear casual. "Hi, Margaret. I heard Billy Barnett was around. I thought I'd say hi if he's in."

"I'm sorry. He left right after lunch."

"That's what I figured, but I thought it was worth a try."

"Don't worry, you'll catch him sometime."

Dylan went out in the hallway and made the call that he'd been dreading.

Sylvester answered on the first ring. "Where the hell were you? I've been calling and calling. It keeps going to voicemail. Didn't you notice?"

"I got tied up."

"Not an answer. If I call you on the phone, you answer the phone. I thought I made that clear."

"I was doing the job everyone at the studio thinks I'm here to do. I couldn't talk."

"So you get away from people and you call me back in two minutes, not two hours. Is that clear?"

"Yes, it is."

"Where is Billy Barnett?"

"He's gone for the day."

There was an ominous pause. **"What did you say?"**

"He had lunch in the cafeteria with some corporate type. Then he left."

"And you didn't follow him?"

"I got tied up in rehearsal."

"What rehearsal? You're not in the damn movie."

"They needed me to prompt the actors."

"You should have got out of it."

"I tried, but the director asked me to be at rehearsal. What was I supposed to do, tell him to go fuck himself? That would be the end of this job."

"So you decided to tell Gino Patelli to go fuck himself. Not a great move. You wanna survive it, stay on the job and do everything in your power to locate Billy Barnett."

Sylvester hung up the phone and went to tell Gino Patelli. He stopped outside the office to straighten his tie and compose himself. He felt just like Dylan must have felt before calling him.

34

Peter called Tessa into his office during one of the rehearsal breaks.

"Hey, Peter, what's up?"

"I just wanted to get your input. How do you think it's going?"

"I think it's going great. Why, is there a problem?"

"Not at all. How do you like working with Viveca?"

"Are you kidding? She's great. Landing her was a real stroke of luck."

"I think so, too. I'm making some script changes, and, like I said in rehearsal, I'm building her part up a little."

"Good idea."

"But I don't want to step on your toes."

"What are you talking about?"

"You know what I mean. You're the star of the movie. I don't want you to feel like I brought in another actress to steal your thunder."

Tessa smiled. "Hey, Peter, it's me. I'm not some actress you have to handle. Anything that helps the movie helps us all. Viveca is nailing her part. Any way you can build it up is fine with me."

Sandy was on cloud nine. The assignments for the shoot had been posted on the wall outside the production office. The production assistants all crowded around to see where they would be working; Sandy was assigned to the set.

"I'm on location!" he crowed. "I knew I was going to be, but you never believe it until it happens. It's not all seniority. I mean, Michael's been here longer than I have, and he's in the studio."

"I asked to stay in the studio," Michael said.

Dylan wasn't surprised. Michael was a computer nerd who was happier programming schedule changes than dealing with real people.

Not that Sandy gave a damn about Michael, but

he had other reasons to be happy about the list. Stacy was also on set.

And Dylan wasn't.

"Bummer, man," Sandy said, "but it was a lot to expect when you're so new."

"Yeah."

"But it doesn't mean we can't celebrate," he added, with the gracious largesse of a winner. "We're all going out. Come on, I'll buy you a beer."

"I wouldn't want to be a wet blanket," Dylan said. "I'm beat, and I'm going home."

Dylan had to get away and call Sylvester, though he was dreading it. Sylvester would go through the roof. On the other hand, Sylvester was already mad about losing Billy Barnett, so how much worse could it be? Dylan figured he might as well give him the bad news all at once.

While the other production assistants trooped out the door on their way to the bar, Dylan slipped down the hall and jerked his cell phone out of his pocket.

"Yes?" Sylvester snapped, so viciously that Dylan almost reconsidered his plan.

"We got production assignments for the shoot. Bad news: Billy Barnett will be on the set, but I won't."

"You what?!"

"I'm not on the set. They assigned me to the

studio. They'll be filming in downtown L.A., but I'll be at Centurion. But it's all right. I'll be on top of things, and I'll be able to tell you exactly where they are."

"I don't want to know where they are. I want to know where Billy Barnett is. I want a firsthand, eyes-on account of exactly where the guy is every moment he's there. Is that clear?"

"It's clear, but there's nothing I can do about it."

"Swap with somebody."

"I can't do that."

"Why not?"

"It isn't done. The production manager wouldn't let me."

"Why does he need to know?"

"He's the boss. He knows where we are and what we're doing."

"Would he take a bribe?"

"No, he would not. If you try something like that, you're just going to make him wise."

"Too bad. You're just going to have to get someone to switch."

"No one is going to be willing to switch, it's a plumb assignment. Look, I'm doing the best I can. If you're not happy, I'll give you back the five hundred dollars you put up for my fine just as soon as I get paid. But there's nothing I can do. I'm tired, I'm pissed off, and I'm going home to get some sleep."

Dylan hung up the cell phone and turned it off. He'd had it with these guys. He was willing to do anything within reason, but this was beyond all bounds. It was an unfortunate set of circumstances. He couldn't see any way out. Maybe if he just stopped his mind and got some rest he'd wake up with a new perspective on life and be able to figure out something to do.

Dylan came out the main gate of Centurion. He considered splurging on a taxi but decided he couldn't do that, not if he wanted to save up the five hundred bucks to pay for his fine. Instead, he took the three long bus rides it took to get home to his one-room, third-floor walk-up apartment. He trudged up the stairs, probably the glummest young man who had ever spent the day hanging out with two beautiful actresses. He unlocked the door and went in.

Strong arms gripped him from behind. A hand was clapped over his mouth. He was lifted off the floor, there was pressure on his chest, and it felt as if his lungs had collapsed.

A light clicked on. Dylan found himself gasping for breath in the clutches of two huge goons.

Sylvester stood in front of him. He didn't look angry. He looked calm.

It was the most chilling thing Dylan had ever seen.

....

So," Sylvester said, "we seem to have a problem. That's all right. Problems come up, then they have to be solved. You disagree. You seem to think problems are to be lived with, that they absolve you of your responsibility. You are wrong. Problems give you the responsibility of solving them. Now, tell me about your problem. You were not picked to be on the set?"

"No."

"Who was picked instead?"

"Sandy."

"Who is Sandy?"

"A guy I work with."

"Then the situation is easy. You will take Sandy's spot."

"I can't do that."

"Why not?"

"He won't give it up."

"Actually, he will. I can help you out in that respect."

"You're going to threaten him?"

"Certainly not. Our presence cannot be known."

Sylvester took out of his pocket a small glass vial full of liquid. He handed it to Dylan.

"What's this?" Dylan said.

Sylvester smiled. "I'm glad you asked."

36

The party was in full swing by the time Dylan got to the bar. Sandy had had a few, and was loud and uninhibited. He spotted Dylan from across the room and bellowed, "Hey, look what the cat dragged in. I told you he couldn't stay away."

Dylan waved and made his way over.

Stacy greeted him warmly. "Glad you could make it."

Sandy's good nature vanished for a second. "Thought you were going home," he said to Dylan.

"I felt like a poor sport, not celebrating with you guys. Let me buy you a drink. What'll you have?"

"Draft beer."

"You got it."

"Get a pitcher."

A pitcher did not suit Dylan's needs, but there was no help for it. He went to the bar and ordered a pitcher, paid, and brought it back to the table.

"Here you go, guys." Dylan filled Sandy's glass first and said, "Who needs a refill?"

Several did. Dylan filled glasses around the table and found the pitcher nearly gone.

Sandy had already chugged half his beer. That was a break. Dylan sat down, dropping the pitcher beneath the top of the table. With his left hand he pulled out the vial and poured it in.

"And here's the man I bought it for," he said, slapping Sandy on the back. He poured the rest of the beer into Sandy's half-filled glass.

"And what are **you** drinking?" Stacy said.

Dylan looked surprised. "Me? I forgot about me."

Everybody laughed.

Dylan took the pitcher back to the bar. He was afraid if he left it someone might try to drink the dregs.

"You want another?" the bartender said.

"Yeah, but not in this. It's got flat beer in it. Give me a new pitcher and let me have my own glass."

"You got it."

Dylan went back to the table, filled his own glass, and set the pitcher down. "Fight over it," he said. "This time I'm taking care of me." He took a slug of beer and stole a glance at Sandy.

Sandy's beer was half full. This time Dylan didn't top it off. If he kept diluting it, Sandy would never finish the dose.

Not to worry. Sandy drained his glass and reached for the pitcher.

Fifteen minutes later Sandy could barely keep his head off the table. His speech was slurred, and his eyelids drooped.

"My drinking buddy's had enough," Dylan said. "I guess that's my fault. I shouldn't have bought those pitchers. Well, I wasn't staying anyway. I'll see he gets home."

Dylan put his arms under Sandy's shoulders and pulled him to his feet.

"I'll help you," Stacy said, getting up from the table.

"Absolutely not," Dylan said. "If he wakes up and finds out the two of us took him home, that is going to have all kinds of bad implications as far as he is concerned."

It wasn't easy, but Dylan managed to get Stacy to sit back down. Then he maneuvered Sandy in an unsteady stumble toward the door.

It was dark out. The sidewalk was empty. A cab came down the street, but Dylan didn't hail it.

Instead, he guided Sandy along the sidewalk into the shadows away from the streetlamp.

A couple of doors down Dylan found what he was looking for: A long stone stairway down the side of the building to a path below.

"Careful," Dylan said, walking Sandy to the top of the steps. "Stand up straight, get your balance. Take care."

Dylan stuck out a foot and gave Sandy's shoulder a little push.

Sandy hurtled through the air and tumbled down the stairs, landing at the bottom in a misshapen heap.

37

Dylan called Hal from the hospital.

"Hal? Dylan. Sorry to call you at home, but there's been an accident. Sandy broke his leg."

"How the hell did that happen?"

"He lost his balance and fell down a flight of stairs."

"Drunk?"

"You know how it is. He was celebrating getting assigned to the set."

"How bad is it?"

"I don't know. They're taking him into surgery now."

"You're at the hospital?"

"Yeah. I rode with him in the ambulance.

Anyway, he wanted me to call you. He knew you'd be upset. You're about to start shooting and he goes and does this."

"Hey, accidents happen. Tell him to take it easy, will you?"

"I'm sure he'll be back on his feet in no time."

"On crutches, you mean. All right, you're going to have to fill in for him. Check the call sheet. Where it says Sandy, that's you. Show up on location, six o'clock Monday morning."

"You got it."

Dylan hung up and called Sylvester.

"I'm in."

38

Early Monday morning, **Trial by Fire** began filming outside the First National Bank in downtown Los Angeles.

For his first shot, Peter had chosen the scene of Viveca walking Tessa into the bank. There were many scenes outside the bank, but Peter had opted to start with that one for many reasons. It was short and simple, just the two women walking into the bank. It was a non-dialogue scene, and could have even been shot without sound, though tape would be rolling. And the actresses were pros who would probably nail it in one take. Getting the first shot always made the crew feel good and started the movie off on the right foot.

The other reason was that Billy Barnett was able to be there because Mark Weldon wasn't in the scene.

Teddy showed up on the set as Mark Weldon, wished the actresses well, and announced cheerily that if anyone needed him he'd be in his trailer.

Teddy's trailer was a new perk, and very welcome. Peter had wanted to give Teddy a trailer all along, but a supporting player rating a trailer would have raised suspicions. A Golden Globe and an Oscar nomination changed all that.

Mark Weldon's trailer was parked on the street right next to Viveca's and Tessa's trailers. Teddy went in and locked the door, in case some eager-beaver assistant director showed up to summon him to the set.

Teddy kicked off his sneakers, pulled off his slacks and polo shirt, and selected a suit and tie from the closet. Then he sat down at the makeup table, opened up his kit, and turned himself into Billy Barnett.

Teddy unlocked the trailer door and peered out. Nobody seemed to be paying any attention. He stepped out of the trailer and headed for the set, stopping to glad-hand any crew members he met on the way. Grips, electricians, propmen, teamsters, Teddy knew them all, and they knew him. Billy Barnett was a workingman's producer who pitched in with the crew, listened to their bitches and moans, and helped in any way he could. During a rough setup he might say to one of the grips, "Can I help you lift this, or would it fuck up some union rule?" Just the offer would ease the tension, make the job go smoothly.

Before he was halfway to the set, Teddy found himself at the caterer's table, having coffee with the gaffer, the key grip, and the teamster captain.

39

Dylan was assigned to traffic control. He wore a headset and had a walkie-talkie, and was one of the production assistants in charge of keeping the crowd behind the rope line.

When the camera rolled, he would be responsible for stopping pedestrian traffic on the sidewalk that Tessa and Viveca had to cross in order to get into the bank.

Down the block the cameramen were lining up the shot, and Peter was coaching Tessa and Viveca on how he wanted the scene. The electricians were setting up reflectors, grips were placing sandbags, and the assistant directors were instructing the extras who would be on the sidewalk.

A propman walked by and headed for the caterer's table, where coffee, bagels, and doughnuts had
been laid out. Dylan wondered if he had time to get
a cup of coffee himself. He'd been there since early
morning, and he hadn't gotten much sleep, what
with hanging out at the hospital with Sandy. He
glanced over at the catering table and saw—

Billy Barnett.

There he was, large as life, holding a paper cup
of coffee and talking to the head electrician. The
gaffer, Sandy had called him. Dylan had a flash
of guilt, thinking of Sandy. He pushed it from his
mind. He needed to focus, save himself, and get
out of this nightmare.

Dylan whipped out his cell phone and called
Sylvester. "He's here."

"Billy Barnett."

"Yes."

"Where?"

"At the caterer's cart, talking to the gaffer."

"The who?"

"The head electrician."

"Good. Don't do anything to tip him off. I'll
take it from here."

The line clicked dead.

Take it from here? Sylvester would take it from
here. What the hell did that mean?

Dylan had a feeling he didn't want to know.

. . . .

Sylvester called Max. "Where are you?"

"Hanging out on the sidewalk with everybody else. Just another starstruck tourist."

Max's account was not entirely accurate. Most of the tourists were in shirtsleeves. Max wore a suit jacket to hide his shoulder holster.

"Good. Barnett's there, at the catering table."

"I'm closer to the camera. It's gotta be down that way. Hang on, let me see."

Max pushed his way through the crowd. He saw several of the crew standing around a table on the sidewalk.

"Wait a minute, wait a minute. There's some guys drinking coffee. Yeah, that's him. He looks just like his picture."

"Take him out."

"That's a problem. There's too many people around."

"They won't see what happened. You lose yourself in the crowd."

"You're not hearing me. There's too many people. I'd have to be standing right next to him. Don't worry, he won't be at the coffee cart forever. I'm on him."

"Just get it done."

Max clicked the phone off, moved in closer to

his prey. His gun was still in his shoulder holster. He wouldn't take it out until he was ready to shoot.

The crowd thinned out. Billy Barnett crumpled up his cup and tossed it in the garbage. Max eased his gun out of his shoulder holster.

A cop walked up, attracted by the doughnuts. He startled Max, made him miss a beat. Billy Barnett began walking away. Max hid his gun under his jacket and started off after his prey.

Billy Barnett was headed for the spot where the camera was set up, right where Max would have been if Sylvester hadn't told him to move.

There came three blasts of a loud buzzing sound, as if someone were ringing a giant telephone. A kid in a headset stepped out on the sidewalk and blocked Max's path.

"Quiet, please. We're on bells. That means were about to shoot a scene. Stay where you are. No talking, please."

Billy Barnett hadn't stopped. He walked right down the sidewalk and greeted the director and the two actresses. Max could see him joking with them a bit before putting up his hands, clearly saying sorry, he knew they were about to shoot, he'd be a good boy, though no one appeared upset at the interruption.

Once again they were ready for the shot.

The assistant director said, "Roll it!"

The sound mixer said, "Speed!"

An assistant cameraman stepped out with a clapboard, said "Scene 46A, take one," and clacked the slate.

The assistant director yelled, "Background, action!"

A few extras walked down the sidewalk.

The director yelled, "Action!"

The two actresses crossed the sidewalk and went into the bank.

"Cut!" the director yelled.

One long bell rang, signaling that the shot was over and people could move again.

Max pushed forward, but he lost sight of Billy Barnett in the crowd. By the time he got to the camera, the producer was gone. So were the actresses, who had been escorted back to their trailers by the assistant directors assigned to their care. Only the director remained. He seemed to be talking to the cameraman about lining up the next shot.

But the producer was nowhere to be seen. Where the hell had he gone? There was a lot of activity around the coffee cart. Max checked it out, but Billy Barnett was not there.

Max's cell phone rang.

It was Sylvester. "Is it done?"

"No, it's not done. They shot a scene and no one would let me get close."

"Are they still shooting it?"

"No, but when it was over there was a huge scrunch of people, and the guy isn't there."

"Find him."

Max never did. About twenty minutes later they had the camera moved, and were ready to film another shot. The actresses came back, along with an actor who was in the scene with them, but the producer never showed.

Teddy, rehearsing the scene as character actor Mark Weldon, kept an eye on the goon in the crowd. He'd spotted him back at the coffee cart, and done his best to keep away from him and avoid making a scene. An ugly incident during the first day's shooting was not the type of publicity Peter needed to launch his movie. Teddy probably would have been able to handle the situation, could have lured Max away from the set and overpowered him when no one was looking, but it wasn't necessary. Teddy knew who he was and who he worked for. It was easier to leave him frustrated than to deal with him right now.

40

Viveca went back to her trailer where her automatic coffeemaker was set to go. She made herself a cup of cappuccino and sat at the table in her little dinette. She sipped the coffee, and took out her cell phone.

"Manny?"

"Hi, Viveca. I hear your picture is doing well."

"Where do you hear that?"

"Industry buzz. You and your costar are getting along, or is that just Hollywood hype?"

"She's not my costar, Manny. I'm just a supporting player."

"You're never a supporting player, no matter what the role. Are you girls playing nice?"

"We're getting along just fine. I like her. That doesn't mean I don't want to beat her on Oscar night."

"What do you need?"

"Oh, I don't know. Maybe just a hint that little Miss Goody Two-shoes is a trifle fond of the bottle."

"She's drunk in rehearsal?"

"I'm not saying that. I want that implied, but I am certainly not the one saying that."

"I can do it. Are you sure you want it?"

"Why not?"

"With so much good publicity coming out, are you sure you want anything negative?"

"As long as it doesn't stick to me."

"It never does."

Gino Patelli was listening to Ollie Fox, one of his underbosses, report on his collection of protection money from the south side. It had been light lately, and Gino had called his boss in to account. Ollie Fox was, despite his name, someone Gino had considered too dumb to steal. He was not, however, too dumb to be stolen **from**, and Gino suspected some of his minions had been skimming.

The conversation was not profitable. Fox had no idea who might have been skimming, and Gino soon lost interest in listening to a man whose underlings were hoodwinking him. When Fox was finally gone, Sylvester, who had been sitting in on the conversation, said, "What do you want to do?"

"Figure out who's stealing the most, dump Fox, and put him in charge. I'd rather have a sharp thief than an idiot. Speaking of which."

"Billy Barnett?"

"Why do you say it like that?"

"Why is it so important?"

"Because he's a ghost," Gino said. "That's what makes him so goddamned interesting. Here's this schmuck movie producer I ought to be able to whack any day of the week, and it's a huge fucking project, and I want to know why."

"It could be just bad luck."

"Bad luck for me, and bad luck for my uncle. Anyone this guy encounters has bad luck. He surfaces just long enough to cause me trouble and disappears again."

"Even so."

"Even so, I'm obsessing about the son of a bitch. It seems like I can't trust anyone else, I gotta handle this myself. So you tell me: How can I get close to Billy Barnett?"

Sylvester considered. "I suppose you could get into the film business," he said facetiously.

Gino cocked his head, and pointed at him. "Let's do that."

Bradley Finch wasn't glad to get the call. Carlo Gigante had helped him out way back when, when Bradley was first trying to get into movies. Bradley owed a lot to Carlo Gigante. But Carlo Gigante was dead, and while Bradley would never say it, it was a bit of a relief now that he was well established in the movie industry as an independent producer who had worked at the major studios. Gigante was a bit of an embarrassment to have in the background, the type of connection a gossip mag might be inclined to publish. So Bradley was glad to be rid of the obligation.

It never occurred to him it might be inherited.

The summons to Gino Patelli's had come as a shock. So had the pat down before he was permitted to enter. Now he sat in the mobster's den with a cigar and a glass of cognac, chatting with Patelli as if they were the best of buddies.

"Of course I knew your uncle," Bradley said. "Great man. Shame what happened to him."

"Yes, it was," Gino said. "But I'm happy he was able to help you get where you are. That's true, isn't it, not just one of the stories people tell?"

"When I was first coming up, Carlo was very helpful."

"I know he was. The way I understand it, he

didn't know that much about the business, but he still had influence."

"That's right."

"I don't know that much about the business," Gino said. "I'd like to, only I don't have my uncle to teach me. But I have you."

"I beg your pardon?"

"You know the industry inside and out. If I wanted to get into producing, what would I have to do?"

"Are you serious?"

"Do you think I brought you here to fuck around?"

"No, no, of course not. You want a shortcut?"

Gino smiled. "Now you're on my wavelength. What would I have to do?"

"Put up money."

"What?"

"You want to become a producer, put up money. I happen to know of a film being financed by an independent studio that's short of cash."

"How much money?"

"Depends how much work you wanna do."

"I don't wanna do any fucking work at all."

"A million dollars. Give them a million dollars, they'll kiss your ass, call you a producer, welcome you on the set. You want a shortcut into the movies, that's the way."

Gino smiled and pointed at Bradley. "I'm beginning to see what Carlo saw in you. So, here's the favor you will do for me, in exchange for the favor my uncle did for you.

"You will find me a movie to invest in. Introduce me to the people I need to know, and help me make it happen.

"Then you will check out the people throwing Oscar parties. Find one who's invited the producer and director of the Centurion movie, **Desperation at Dawn**. That shouldn't be hard, it's an Oscar nominee. Get me an invite to that party."

Bradley stared at Gino, his mouth open. "Are you serious?"

"You do that, and we will consider the debt paid."

"I'm glad to hear it," Bradley said. He hoped Gino wouldn't consider that sarcastic. "This will take some time. When do you need it done?"

Gino shrugged. "How's tomorrow?"

There's **another** Oscar party?" Teddy said. "How many of these damn things are there?"

"You knew about it," Peter said.

"That doesn't mean I like it. Couldn't we skip this one?"

"We have to go," Peter said.

"Robert Vincent? I've never even heard of the guy."

"That's why we have to go. He's not on the A-list. If we snub him, it will look like we think we're too big for him."

"Do people really think like that?" Teddy said.

Peter looked at him.

Teddy spread his arms. "What am I saying? Of course people think like that."

"I knew you'd understand."

"So who's he inviting, Mark Weldon or Billy Barnett?"

"Both."

"So who's going to snub him?"

"Well, it's a problem either way. A no-show will be noticed by Oscar voters."

"It's easy then. Billy Barnett will go. Mark Weldon couldn't care less if he wins an Oscar."

"It all reflects on the picture."

"I think you want to win an Oscar."

Peter grinned. "Bite your tongue."

"Okay, I'll go as Billy Barnett. I'll catch a ride with you to the party because my car's still in the shop."

"It is?"

"Well, it's probably done, I just haven't picked it up. Have a production assistant drop off a car at the party and give you the keys. You slip me the keys when no one's looking. Then after every Oscar voter in Southern California has a chance to see that Billy Barnett is just a regular guy, I'll take off in the car, change into Mark Weldon, and come back."

"That sounds complicated," Peter said.

"Yeah. It would be easier if Billy Barnett had a cold."

"Not that complicated."

It was quite a party. Cars were parked by the side of the road for a hundred yards in both directions. Policemen had been hired to direct traffic, as cars were allowed to pull up to the front door momentarily to let off the rich and famous.

Teddy caught a ride in Ben Bacchetti's limo, along with Ben, Tessa, Peter, and Hattie. Teddy was there as Billy Barnett. He figured it was easier to put in an appearance as the producer first, and let the actor come fashionably late.

Robert Vincent met him at the door. They had never been introduced, but that didn't stop Robert from greeting him effusively as if they were old friends.

"I have to congratulate you on your success. It must be wonderful to have an Oscar contender."

Teddy smiled. "It's easy to produce a hit picture. Just let Peter Barrington direct."

"Ah, Peter Barrington," Robert gushed, continuing to fawn over everyone in the group.

Teddy couldn't recall what Robert Vincent had

produced himself. He had a feeling the man was more successful at producing parties than movies.

Viveca Rothschild was already there. Teddy spotted her across the room. He made his way toward her and greeted her warmly. She was in the company of a muscular young man she introduced as her boyfriend, Bruce. Teddy would have known he was ex-military without being told. Bruce had a look he sometimes recognized in soldiers who had been under fire.

"Glad to see you," Viveca said. "You're so seldom around."

"One of the drawbacks of success," Teddy said. "I find I'm working on more than one project at a time. Believe me, though, I'm keeping tabs on your film. If I'm not on the scene all the time, it's actually a good thing. When a movie's going well, there's nothing to worry about."

"All her movies go well," Bruce said.

It was an aggressive comment, about what Teddy would have expected from the young man, and it almost forced Viveca to say something self-deprecating to mitigate it.

Before she could, Teddy said, "I've seen her movies, and I quite agree. Nice to meet you, young man."

....

On the other side of the room, Gino Patelli and Sylvester were sipping drinks and keeping an eye on Billy Barnett, whom they had spotted when he came in. As Billy moved away from Viveca and Bruce, Gino weaved his way through the crowd and intercepted him.

"Billy Barnett. An Oscar contender." He extended his hand. "Allow me to offer my congratulations."

"Thank you," Teddy said. "Pardon me, but have we met?"

"No, we have not. Gino Patelli. I'm a producer myself."

Teddy's CIA training allowed him not to react to the name, but it was certainly interesting. So, this was Carlo Gigante's nephew, the man who had tried several times to have him killed. Instinct told Teddy he had nothing to fear from him here. Gino wouldn't do his own dirty work, and the man with him wouldn't do anything that might reflect on his boss. Teddy was safe at the party.

He was sure he wouldn't be when he left.

"Pleased to meet you, Mr. Patelli. What have you produced?"

"I'm doing a picture now for Allied Films. Looks like a winner. This is my associate, Sylvester. We're relatively new to the business. I was hoping you might have some advice."

"Start with the script," Teddy said. "Most people say get a star. Line up a big-name actor, build around that. But for my money they're wrong. You put a star actor in a turkey, you got a movie no one wants to see. Start with the script, let the script attract the star." He smiled. "Sorry, that's more than you want to hear. It's just one of my pet peeves."

"Not at all," Gino said. "That's very helpful. You've given me something to think about."

Teddy drained his glass, which gave him an excuse to move away to get another drink.

Gino had given him something to think about, too. For all of Gino's macho posturing, he struck Teddy as a little boy, dressed up in his uncle's clothing, trying to be a man. He cared very much about his image. He did not want anyone to get the impression he had failed. Having gone after Billy Barnett, he could not let the vendetta go, even to the point of dabbling in the motion-picture industry to accomplish his ends. The man was irrational, psychotic, and extremely dangerous. Eventually, he would have to be dealt with.

The tinkling of a piano piece cut through the conversation and gradually quieted the crowd. Hattie Barrington had been prevailed upon to grace the company with a selection from her Oscar-nominated score. It was gorgeous. Even the bare piano notes hinted at the arrangement the full orchestra could deliver. Her piece was greeted with appreciative applause.

Teddy mingled for about an hour, worked his way over to Peter, and said, "It's time. See you later."

They shook hands, and Peter palmed him the car keys.

Teddy thanked his host and headed for the door. Out of the corner of his eye he could see Gino Patelli talking on his cell phone. He had a feeling he knew what that was about.

43

Teddy came out the front door. He couldn't see Gino's men, but he knew they were there. He figured they wouldn't try to take him out in the doorway. The police presence was enough to keep him safe, unless he walked alone to his car.

One of the cops was waiting in the driveway to deal with the late arrivals. Teddy waved him over.

"Can you do me a favor? A production assistant left a car for me to get home with. It's parked up the road to the right. I got a bum leg, and I'd rather not walk. Could you drive it up here for me?"

Teddy extended the keys and a fifty-dollar bill.

The cop smiled. "To the right, you say?" He took the keys and the bill and set off.

Teddy stepped back inside and waited for the car to drive up. He doubted if Gino's men would risk a long shot, but he saw no reason to give them a chance.

The cop drove up with the production car. Teddy hopped in, perhaps too athletically for someone with a bad leg, not that it mattered. A producer might well tell a white lie to disguise that he was too lazy to get his own car.

Teddy drove quickly out of the Hollywood hills to a commercial strip alongside the highway. He built up a lead, then turned abruptly into a cheap motel. Instead of parking in front of the units, he pulled into the shadows on the far side of the lot, hopped out, sprinted across the parking lot, and went in the door of unit 10 just as headlights turned in off the road.

That was cutting it close, but even so. With luck they wouldn't know what unit he was in.

Teddy double-locked the motel room door, went to the closet, and took out the change of clothes he'd left there earlier that afternoon when he'd rented the unit. He slipped off his suit jacket, hung it on a hanger, and changed into the sportier but still dressy attire he'd chosen for Mark Weldon. He took his makeup kit out of a dresser drawer, went into the bathroom, and began the transformation. Minutes later, Mark Weldon's face stared back at him. Teddy shot him with his finger, a jaunty gesture suitable for the stuntman actor.

Teddy opened the motel room safe and took out his gun and shoulder holster. It would have been inappropriate for Billy Barnett, but for bad boy Mark Weldon it was a signature prop. On the off chance anyone spotted it, they wouldn't even be sure it was real.

Teddy went to the window and peered out through a crack in the blinds. He could see two men skulking behind his car. That was unfortunate. He could ditch them, but they might have seen him go into the room as Billy Barnett. When they saw him come out as Mark Weldon, it wouldn't take a genius to put two and two together.

Teddy went in the bathroom and checked the window. It was large, as motel bathroom windows go. He unlocked it, pushed it open, and carefully lifted out the screen. He stepped on the toilet seat and climbed out the window.

Behind the motel was relatively dark. Only two of the bathroom lights were on. Teddy faded back into the shadows and detoured around the building.

He reached the end of the row farthest from the road. Here the motel angled into an L. Teddy worked his way to the end of the units, and peered around the corner.

The two thugs were still crouched in the darkness behind his car. One was of average height, the other was short and stocky. Short and Stocky already had his gun out. He would be nervous and apt to fire at the slightest provocation. Average Height would be less apt to miss.

Teddy took his gun out and screwed on the silencer. He kept in the shadows and tried to work his way around behind them.

A twig snapped.

Short and Stocky reacted as if it were a gunshot. He whirled around, leveled his gun.

Teddy shot him in the head. He went down in a heap.

Average Height went for his gun. Too late, way too late. Teddy put two in his chest as he turned, one in his head before he could shoot.

Teddy searched their pockets. Average Height had a set of car keys. He zapped them. Lights flashed on a car parked on the same side of the lot just two spaces away.

Teddy grabbed Short and Stocky under the shoulders, dragged him to the car, popped the trunk, and dropped him in. Then he went back for his partner.

. . . .

Max was crouched between the cars parked in front of units 7 and 8. It was a perfect vantage place. If Billy Barnett came out of the motel, Max would be able to sneak up behind him. Billy Barnett might be smart, but he would never know what hit him.

It was a shock to realize Billy Barnett hadn't done that.

Max was focused on the motel when he heard the unmistakable **pop** of silenced gunshots somewhere behind him. He turned just in time to see his cronies going down.

Lights on their car flashed. Billy Barnett had their keys. Shadows moved in the dark, then a light flared as he popped the trunk. Max saw a clump of figures as Billy rolled a body inside.

It was time to make his move. Billy Barnett clearly didn't know he was there. He would be dealing with the second body, and wouldn't be alert for an attack, particularly from the direction of the motel.

Max slipped from between the cars and crossed the lot. There was one car parked between Billy Barnett's and the one with the open trunk. Max crept to it, flattened his back against it, and waited. He felt good. Another minute and the job would be over. He'd lost his partners, but that wasn't his problem. Gino would be pleased.

Max raised his gun.

Billy Barnett did not appear. It took a moment for it to register on Max that the footsteps had stopped. His eyes widened with the realization just before the bullet tore into the back of his head.

44

When Teddy got back to the party Gino Patelli was making frequent phone calls. They appeared to be going straight to voicemail. He didn't look happy.

Teddy greeted the host, then headed for the Centurion contingent, where Viveca and Bruce had joined Peter and Hattie and Ben and Tessa.

"You're late," Viveca said with a smile. "Is that part of your bad-boy image?"

Teddy grinned. "Hey, I'm not pretty like you. I have to work to get attention."

Viveca laughed. She got along well with Mark, and was comfortable kidding him.

Her boyfriend stiffened at the familiarity. Teddy

allowed himself to be introduced to Bruce again. "Oh, firm handshake. You're a vet, aren't you? Can always spot a military man. Pleased to meet you. Well, you guys got a head start on me. I'm going to get a drink."

Teddy wandered over to the bar.

Tessa followed him. "Is everything all right?"

"Sure. What'll you have?"

"Oh. A martini."

"One martini and one bourbon on the rocks," Teddy said.

The bartender mixed the drinks.

"You took your time getting back," Tessa said.

"I was in no rush to be here."

"What aren't you telling me?"

Teddy just smiled.

Tessa leaned in close. "Hey, it's me. I know when something's going on. What is it?"

"Nothing to do with you. And nothing to do with Mark Weldon. So there's no reason not to enjoy ourselves."

Teddy accepted the drinks from the bartender. He handed Tessa the martini. "There you go." He raised his glass. "To the Oscars," he said. "Someone's gotta win 'em. Might as well be us."

They clinked glasses.

Tessa took a sip.

A cell phone camera clicked.

45

Ben Bacchetti was livid. "How did this happen?" he said. He waved the newspaper aloft and pointed at the picture. It showed Tessa Tweed at the Oscar party laughing and hoisting a martini. The headline of the article read: TIPSY TWEED?

"How does this even happen?" Ben said. "This is from the party. This was taken last night. Did you even see a camera there?"

"It's from a cell phone photo," Teddy said.

"That's very clear."

"It's been enhanced."

"You mean photoshopped? Someone mocked it up?"

"It's not mocked up. It's a real photograph. I know when it was taken."

"When?"

"Last night when I went to the bar. Tessa came over. I got her a drink and handed it to her. We toasted the Oscars. That's what you see there."

"Do you think someone was planted at the party to take that picture?"

"Or happened to be there and saw a chance to make some extra cash."

"Yeah, but look at this," Ben said, pointing to the newspaper. "It's like the guy wrote the article and then shot a photo to go with it."

"No one set the photo up. If the host had caught them, that would be their last invitation anywhere."

"I suppose," Ben conceded.

"So what do you want to do?"

"This reporter who wrote the story," Ben said. "It's the same one who wrote the others. This Josh Hargrove. I want to have a little talk with him."

"No, you don't," Teddy said.

"The hell I don't."

"This is a small story. It isn't true, but that's the least of it. It's boring. Tessa Tweed had a drink at a party? Ho-hum. But if you fly off the handle and attack this reporter, it's a huge story. It's big and it's fun and it's news. That's why the paparazzi hound celebrities. If they can get them to react, they've got something. If they can't, they don't."

"Well, something needs to be done," Ben said. "This can't go on forever."

"I know."

"So what do you suggest?"

"Let me talk to him," Teddy said.

46

Teddy called Josh Hargrove at the **Culver City Chronicle**, and wasn't surprised to find the reporter wasn't there. Hargrove was a stringer and worked out of his apartment.

Teddy called him at home. "Josh Hargrove? You write for the **Chronicle**, right? I got a hot tip for you."

"Oh?"

"I know, I know, everyone's giving you tips. Most of them are crap. I'm the real deal. I'll give you a tip, and if you don't want it, you don't use it, no hard feelings. If you write it, you give me what you think's fair, and we got a working relationship."

"What's the tip?"

"It's hard for you to pay me over the phone, no? Let's meet."

"Fine." Josh gave Teddy an address in an old building that had been renovated since the war.

When he arrived, Teddy rode up in the refurbished elevator to apartment 14F.

Josh let him in but didn't invite him to sit down.

"What's the tip?"

"Tessa Tweed was drinking at an Oscar party."

Hargrove frowned. "That's in the paper."

"Yes, it is. Who gave you **that** tip?"

"None of your business. You got a tip for me or not?"

"Yes, I do. Stop writing about Tessa Tweed."

Hargrove scowled. "I'm going to ask you to leave."

"When?"

"What?"

"When are you going to ask me?"

"I'm asking you now," Josh cried in exasperation.

"Yeah, but you're so wishy-washy about it. Afraid to make a definitive statement. But let's assume you asked me to leave. I'm not going to. So, who gave you the story?"

"I can't reveal my sources."

"Of course you can. We've already established you have no ethics. We're not in a courtroom. There's nothing legal about this. It's just you and me. And I'm asking you to tell me who gave you the story. And you're going to do it because you're a coward, and you always take the coward's way out."

"Now, see here."

"Oh, don't make up any more bullshit. You're not writing these stories because you want to. You're writing them because you have to. Someone scared you, and you're more scared of them than you are of me. We need to flip that."

Teddy looked out one of the living room windows. It was the old-fashioned type, with a rickety wood frame and many panes of glass.

Teddy marched to the window and threw it open.

He grabbed the reporter by the scruff of his neck and the seat of his pants and gave him the bum's rush straight at the window as if he were going to throw him out.

Teddy stopped just in time. He smiled at the man and said, "Just kidding."

Before Josh could react, Teddy reached down, grabbed him by the legs, flipped him up, and hung him out the window.

Josh screamed in terror.

Teddy waited for him to subside, then said calmly, "Want me to pull you up?"

"Yes!"

"I thought so," Teddy said. He smiled. "Who gave you the story?"

47

Manny's office was a second-floor walk-up over a coffee shop. Teddy banged on the door, but there was no answer. It was just as well. He was due back on the set to work with Peter and he wouldn't have had time to give the gentleman the attention he deserved.

Teddy drove back to the location, which was still the bank. He parked the production car on the street, tossed the keys to one of the PAs, and slipped into Mark Weldon's trailer when no one was looking. Five minutes later Mark Weldon emerged and headed for the set.

He was shooting a scene with Viveca. She'd been shooting all morning with Tessa and probably could have used a break, but Viveca was a real trouper in that regard. When it was time to get down to work, she was always ready.

So was Teddy. The two of them nailed their scene in one take, and Viveca was done for the day.

Viveca went back to her trailer to change. Before she could, Peter Barrington knocked and poked his head in the door.

"Hi. I know you want to get home, but could you spare a moment?"

"Of course."

"Good. I just wanted to talk to you while they move the camera."

"Is there a problem?"

"Not at all, I couldn't ask for anything better in your performance. You and Tessa are wonderful together."

"It's nice of you to give me lines."

"I'm not being nice. I'm trying to make the best picture possible. You guys are helping me do that, and believe me, it's great."

Viveca laughed. "Well, let's not go overboard. So far all we've done is walk into a bank."

"Yes. A simple action scene that somehow managed to say it all. Anyway, I was just on the horn with Ben Bacchetti, and he has managed to work it out with all concerned. So, if we can just work it out with you and your agent, we're all set."

"Work what out?"

"Well, we originally intended the credits to be: Tessa Tweed in **Trial by Fire**. When you came on we made you the first credit after the title, so it went: Tessa Tweed in **Trial by Fire**, with Viveca Rothschild."

"Which was very nice of you, but Mark has a much bigger part. I hate to edge him out in the credits."

"Believe me, he doesn't mind. He's a glorified stuntman basking in success. He couldn't care less about the credits. He's happy just to be in a movie with you. Anyway, we're moving him to first credit after the titles."

She frowned. "You're bumping me down?"

"Not on your life. If it all works out, we're billing you above the title: Tessa Tweed and Viveca Rothschild in **Trial by Fire**, with Mark Weldon."

"You've got to be kidding me."

"Not at all."

"Does Tessa know about that?"

"It was her idea."

Viveca was stunned. She felt a flash of guilt about trying to tear Tessa down, but reminded herself that her feelings were separate from her professional aims. The Oscar competition was always cutthroat. It had nothing to do with Tessa as a person. It was all the Hollywood game.

And yet . . . Viveca was beginning to wonder if she believed her own bullshit anymore.

48

Manny was in the barbershop when the phone rang. He got barber shaved only occasionally, when he had a little money, and thanks to the Tessa Tweed stories he was flush.

When the phone rang, Manny was lying back in the chair, his face covered with shaving cream, the barber poised over him with a straight razor.

"Aw, hell," Manny said.

"You gonna get that?" the barber said.

"Let it go to voicemail."

Manny waited until he was on his way out the door before checking his voicemail.

The message was from Josh Hargrove, who

sounded hysterical. Manny couldn't make sense of what he'd said. He quickly dialed Josh's number.

"Jesus Christ, where were you? I couldn't reach you."

"You got me now. What is it?"

"The shit's hit the fan. There was a guy here, in my apartment, asking about the Tessa Tweed story. Some producer or other. I gave him your name."

"You gave him my **name**?" Manny said ominously.

"He held me upside down out the fucking window. He was going to kill me, Manny. I swear to God, the guy is unhinged."

"So you gave him my name?"

"That's why I called to warn you. This guy is nuts. I couldn't hold out on him, and you won't be able to either. If I were you, I'd get out of town."

"Good thing you're not me."

"What?"

"Asshole."

Manny slipped the phone back in his pocket and walked around the corner to his office. He unlocked the door and plopped down behind his desk.

Manny kept a bottle in his desk drawer. It had started as a joke, a clichéd prop for his gossip-columnist image, but it soon turned into what it was: a bottle of booze in a desk drawer to ease the end of the day.

It wasn't the end of the day, but it needed easing. Manny took out the bottle, poured himself a shot, and tossed it down.

All right. A producer was coming to shake him down. That wasn't so bad, no matter what Josh Hargrove said. That coward had likely caved when the guy had given him a mean look.

Manny wondered if the producer would try to pay him off, and how much. It was a fleeting thought. He couldn't sell out Viveca without losing a steady stream of income.

But that didn't mean he couldn't turn a profit. It was all a matter of how you looked at things.

Manny picked up the phone and called Viveca.

"Hello, Manny."

"Are you on the set?"

"No, I wrapped early. I'm on my way home."

"Are you alone?"

"Aside from the driver."

"Can he hear you?"

"The glass is up. He can't hear a thing. Why?"

"Josh called. From the **Chronicle**."

"Speaking of Josh, we should ease back on that, I think."

"Yeah, yeah, not the point. He said a guy came to find out who gave him the Tessa Tweed story."

"Did he mention my name?"

"He doesn't know your name. I never gave it to him."

"All right, then—"

"It's not all right. Josh gave him **my** name."

"Why the hell did he do that?"

"He says the guy threatened him. I think he paid him off. The guy's not some goon, he's a producer, for Pete's sake."

Viveca sucked in her breath. "Billy Barnett?"

"That's the one."

"Well, shit."

"What is it?"

"He's producing the picture I'm filming now."

"Well, don't worry about it. I'm not going to give you up. No matter how much money he offers, I won't let you down."

49

Bruce knew at once that something was wrong. He was sometimes slow on the uptake socially, but he'd been with Viveca so long he was sensitive to her moods. "What is it?" he said.

Viveca didn't want to talk about it, particularly not with Bruce. But he wouldn't let things go. He hated the idea that people were talking above his head.

"Nothing, really. Manny called."

"What did he want?"

"Money, actually."

"What?"

"You know he's been doing those stories for me?"

"To help you win the Oscar."

"That's right. He got a reporter to write some stories about Tessa Tweed. A producer from our movie's been trying to find out where the story came from. The reporter didn't know it was me, but he gave up Manny."

"Did Manny give you up?"

"Not yet, but I'm afraid he will. Manny swears he'll keep his mouth shut, and wants more money for the trouble."

"The producer hasn't talked to him yet?"

"No, he hasn't, but he will. I'm afraid Manny will crack and I'll be exposed. The worst part of it is that, aside from wanting to beat Tessa out of the Oscar, I really **like** her. I don't want her to find out I did this. I couldn't bear it. How could I go on working with her? It's just a big mess."

"Manny won't give you up."

"He's not a saint, he's a gossip columnist. He'd sell out his own mother."

"You're all keyed up. Have a drink, sit in the hot tub. Veg out and watch a movie." Bruce hesitated. "I was going to run some errands, but I won't if you don't want to be alone."

Viveca was delighted to be rid of him. She was pouring herself a drink when he went out the door.

Bruce didn't have errands to run. He got in the car, asked Siri for Manny Rosen's address, and took off for downtown L.A.

50

Manny opened the door on a safety chain. He wanted to judge just how angry this producer was before he let him in.

Only it wasn't the producer. It was someone he knew, Viveca's boyfriend. What was he doing here?

Maybe delivering money, a bonus for him keeping quiet under duress. He had known Viveca was clever enough to take the hint.

Manny took off the chain and let the young man in.

"You're Viveca's boyfriend."

"Bruce."

"Right. Bruce. I'm Manny. I think we met at one time or other. So what brings you here?"

"Viveca says there's trouble."

"Nothing serious, someone asking about a story and she doesn't want her name mentioned. I assure you it won't be. Just as I assured her."

"She's still worried."

"So she sent me some money? It wasn't necessary, but she's made her point. Whatever someone offers me, she'll go higher. I know that, and she knows I know that. But I'm happy for the reminder. It's a show of good faith."

"Yeah, yeah, whatever."

Bruce wandered over to Manny's desk. It was bare save for a telephone, a bottle of booze, a pen, a pad of paper, a letter opener, and some mail.

Bruce turned back and leaned against the side of the desk, his eyes on Manny.

Manny was getting a little exasperated with the kid. He remembered hearing he was a little slow. "So, you got something for me or not?"

"Oh, I got something for you," Bruce said.

He picked up the letter opener and, with the brutal efficiency learned in the army, plunged it into the gossip columnist's heart.

51

When Teddy finished shooting for the day, he went back to his trailer and transformed into Billy Barnett. He borrowed a production car and drove out to Manny Rosen's office. He parked in front, went up the stairs, and saw that the gossip columnist's door was slightly ajar. Teddy knocked, but there was no response. Teddy stood to the side of the door and cautiously pushed it open. When he still heard nothing from inside, he peeked through the door.

A man was lying facedown on the desk. Teddy went over and checked for a pulse and didn't find one, though he hadn't expected to. Further inspection revealed the man—who Teddy assumed must be Manny—had a letter opener in his heart.

Teddy sighed in disgust. Manny was going to be a poor source of information unless he'd left some clues behind, perhaps in the form of a note or memo.

Teddy removed a handkerchief from his pocket so he could examine the scene without leaving fingerprints. First he emptied the man's pockets. According to his driver's license, the man was, indeed, Manny Rosen, but he had nothing helpful on his person. Nor was there anything helpful on top of his desk.

Teddy eased the desk drawers open, but found nothing of interest except an address book. He set it on the desk and flipped through it, checking the names and phone numbers.

The door flew open and three cops burst into the room, guns drawn.

"All right! Hold it right there!"

52

Stone Barrington and Dino Bacchetti were enjoying dinner at Patroon, their frequent restaurant of choice ever since Elaine's had closed. Stone was enjoying osso buco, Dino rack of lamb.

They were just finishing up their entrées and contemplating dessert when a cell phone rang.

"Is that mine?" Stone said.

"It must be," Dino said. "My ringtone plays 'Hail to the Chief.'" Dino Bacchetti was New York City's police commissioner. Since the two men had once been beat cops together, Dino often joked about the importance of his office.

Stone Barrington answered his phone. "Hello?"

"Stone. It's Billy Barnett."

"Hi, Billy. How are you?"

"Is that Billy Barnett?" Dino said. "Say hi for me."

"Thanks, but this isn't a social call," Teddy said. "I'm in jail."

"Are you kidding me?"

"I wish I were. I'm in the L.A. county lockup awaiting arraignment."

"On what charge?"

"Murder."

"Did you do it?"

"Not this time."

"How'd you get arrested?"

"The police found me at the crime scene examining the corpse."

"That's usually what they call 'caught red-handed.'"

"Well, it wasn't what I'd planned to be doing."

"No, I would imagine not."

"Anyway, I'm in a bit of a sticky situation. I was hoping you could recommend a lawyer who could handle it for me."

"You're talking to him."

"Thanks, but that won't work."

"Why not?"

"Peter started filming his latest picture. I don't have a scene tomorrow, but I have to be on the set first thing the following day."

"You should have thought of that before you found a dead guy."

"Thanks, Stone. That's just the type of legal advice I was hoping for."

"Relax. I have no pressing business in New York at the moment. I'll fly out to L.A. and have you out in time for dinner tomorrow."

"I don't think the police will be inclined to let me go."

"I won't deal with the police. I'll deal with the prosecutor. What have they got on you, anyway?"

"I'm not sure they've figured it out yet. So far they just caught me at the scene."

"Did you have a motive to kill the guy?"

"Never met him."

"Then what were you doing there?"

"The guy was a gossip columnist. He was spreading rumors about Tessa Tweed, and I wanted to find his source."

"What kind of rumors?"

"That she's a drunk who can't say her lines right, so her voice had to be dubbed."

"This guy was saying that?"

"Yeah."

"But you didn't kill him?"

"No."

"Why not?"

Stone hung up the phone to find Dino looking at him.

"What's up?" Dino said.

"Billy's accused of killing a gossip columnist for saying nasty things about your daughter-in-law. Care to come to L.A.?"

Dino's eyes blazed. "Try and stop me."

53

ADA Harold Felson wasn't pleased. "It's Hollywood, Stone. We try to accommodate the movie people."

"And I appreciate it."

"But that's no reason to take advantage."

"I wouldn't do that."

"I'm expediting the booking because your client has to be back on the set."

"He does."

"He's a producer, Stone. Not an actor or director. They can roll film without him. He doesn't have to be there. Hell, some producers never show up on the set."

"This one does." Stone lowered his voice. "Cut

me some slack here. It's my son's picture. Billy is his main producer and they work well together. Their last picture just received an Oscar nomination."

"Which one is that?"

"**Desperation at Dawn.**"

"Good picture. Congratulations. But that doesn't mean I won't catch heat. Hollywood producer given the kid-glove treatment."

"I'm not asking for the kid-glove treatment, I'm asking for due process. Charge him or release him and get on with something else."

"'Release him'? Stone, we're talking about a murder."

"You know and I know a Hollywood producer doesn't burst into a gossip columnist's office, stab him to death, and stand there waiting for the police to arrive. And other than Mr. Barnett's presence in Mr. Rosen's office for a scheduled appointment, you've got nothing on him. You're going to have to drop the charge, and that never makes you look good."

"Failing to charge a prime suspect for a murder won't make me look good!"

Stone sighed. "I can bring the full fury of Woodman and Weld down upon you. They'll send a team of attorneys out here to go through every bit of this case with a fine-tooth comb, and I know your case is weak to begin with. You think arresting this producer is a public relations nightmare? Just wait until you're humiliated in the courtroom on a high-profile case."

Harold Felson was speechless for a moment, his mouth opening and closing like a fish. Finally he sputtered, "Stone, you've got to give me something here."

"He was caught in the guy's apartment, right? Charge him with breaking and entering."

54

Judge Hobbs squinted at the docket. "Call the next case."

"Billy Barnett. Breaking and entering."

Teddy stepped forward. Stone was at his side.

"Stone Barrington for the defense, Your Honor."

"ADA Felson for the prosecution."

Judge Hobbs frowned. "This is a simple arraignment."

"Yes, Your Honor."

"I note that the charge was originally murder. Why was it reduced to breaking and entering?"

"Lack of evidence, Your Honor. In the course of the investigation the charge may be amended."

"Or dropped," Stone Barrington added.

Judge Hobbs frowned. "I don't know what's going on here, but by the normal course of events this seems strange. This is a simple arraignment. In light of the reduced charges, I don't assume the prosecution will be resisting bail?"

"No, Your Honor."

"And the defense?"

"We're amenable to dropping the charges or releasing him on his own recognizance. But, barring that, I brought my wallet."

"The defendant poses no flight risk?"

"He's producing a motion picture, Your Honor, and has another nominated for an Academy Award. He's also willing to surrender his passport."

Judge Hobbs considered. "I am willing to release the defendant on nominal bail as long as he does not leave the jurisdiction of the court. Defendant is charged with breaking and entering. Bail is set at five thousand dollars. Mr. Barnett, do not make me regret this."

Nicely done," Teddy said, as Stone posted bail.

"Just routine. In case he didn't go for it, Dino was ready to throw his weight around with the police department."

"Dino has no jurisdiction out here."

"Dino thinks the New York City police commissioner has jurisdiction everywhere. I have to hold him back from cutting in front of kids at the ice cream parlor."

"Where is he now?"

"Scouting out the media. We'd like to get you out of here without running into the paparazzi."

Teddy signed for his possessions. He slipped on his watch and stuffed his keys and wallet into his pockets as Dino came walking up.

"What's the score?" Stone said.

"A couple of reporters on the front steps. We might be able to walk by them, but there's no reason to try. A young detective showed me a back door we can use."

"Do we want to get caught sneaking out a back door?"

"According to him, no one's going to see us."

Stone, Dino, and Teddy took a detour in the lobby, walked by the offices of tax assessors, county clerks, and municipal employees to a secondary lobby and reception area with wide stairs leading down to three double doors to the street.

They walked down the steps and pushed the doors open.

A dozen camera crews mobbed the steps, along

with a horde of reporters shoving microphones and asking questions.

As they fought their way through the mob, Dino muttered, "One young detective is **so** dead."

55

Sylvester could hardly contain himself. "Guess who got arrested?"

"Who?"

"Billy Barnett."

"What for?"

"Murder."

"You framed him for **another** murder?"

"I didn't."

"Someone else framed him for murder?"

"He might have actually done this one."

"What?"

"Turns out he had a motive. Some gossip columnist was spreading nasty rumors about his lead actress."

"He killed him for that?"

"It does seem a bit of an overreaction."

Gino looked at him sharply. "You find this funny?"

"The man's causing us no end of trouble. It's hard not to enjoy his misfortune."

"Where are you getting your information?"

"It's on the news. He was arraigned this morning. The TV stations covered his release."

"How come we didn't get a heads-up?"

"My man on the force was off duty. When I called him it was the first he'd heard of it."

"Where's Barnett now?"

"Supposedly back on the set. I called Dylan, but he hasn't seen him."

Gino slammed his fist down on the desk. "What is it with this guy? He's the original Teflon man. The cops can't get him, we can't get him. He's never where he's supposed to be. You can't pin him down. He gets arrested for murder, and he's out and gone before we even hear. How'd he get out so quick on a murder charge?"

"They charged him with B and E. They can always up the charges, but the defense won't get them kicked for lack of proof. For the prosecutor it's a win-win."

"For Billy Barnett, too. He waltzes in and out

of jail like he owned the place, and completely disappears."

"It would appear so."

"Get ahold of Dylan. If Barnett's not there, he can damn well find out where he is."

Dylan wasn't any help. "He's not here, but that doesn't mean anything. The place is crawling with TV crews. He might be holed up in one of the trailers and ducking the press."

"Nose around, find out where he's hiding."

"There's a limit to how interested I can be without people getting wise."

"Well, then, you'd better be careful, hadn't you?"

56

Teddy scrunched down in the front seat of the Subaru Outback and held a gun to Tessa's head.

"See that?" he said. "Keep watching."

The camera mounted in the back of the station wagon shot their POV through the windshield. Across the street, the front door of the bank opened and a man in a suit and tie came down the steps.

"That's your buddy, isn't it?" Teddy said. "Trey Verdon. Head teller, vying for assistant manager. I wonder how long it would take him to get it."

Viveca came out of the bank and followed Trey Verdon down the street.

"The guy seems like a bit of a twit. Did you like him much?"

"Goddamn it," Tessa said.

Teddy jabbed her with the gun. "And that is what you cannot do. Want him to live? It's up to you." He whipped out a cell phone. "I have only to make the call. Thumbs up or thumbs down? Do I have your total cooperation?"

Tessa looked at Teddy, her expression one of trepidation tinged with determination. The tension was palpable.

"And cut!" Peter Barrington yelled. "Camera one, good for picture?" The operator gave him the okay sign. "Camera two? Camera three? All right, we're going again. Viveca, come in one step sooner or the distance between the two of you is problematic. Do you need a new start cue?"

Viveca smiled. "No, I got it."

"Okay, good. Check makeup and continuity, let's go in five."

Teddy climbed out of the car.

The gofer Dylan spotted him and came over. "Mark. Hey, is Billy Barnett around?"

"Supposed to be, but I haven't seen him. You need something?"

"No, just concerned. All this publicity, I want him to know we're behind him."

Teddy smiled. "It's the movies, kid. If people aren't talking about you, you're doing something wrong."

"Yeah, but murder?"

"Trust me, no one thinks he did it."

Teddy headed for the coffee cart. He hadn't had any sleep and was starting to fade. Luckily the shot Peter had chosen just called for him to be sitting in a car. A more athletic scene might have been iffy.

Teddy dumped milk in his coffee and took a big sip. Down the street he could see the production assistant Dylan. Was the kid's interest in Billy Barnett normal curiosity, or was it something else?

Teddy no sooner had that thought than the actor playing the head teller Trey Verdon slid in next to him at the coffee urn.

"Hey, Mark. You know what's up with Billy Barnett? I heard he was released, but now he's not around?"

Teddy nodded. That was it. Billy Barnett was the main topic of conversation.

Dylan wandered in the direction of Peter's trailer, hoping to catch the young director on his way back to the set and slip in a casual question about Billy Barnett.

Before he got there, the trailer door opened and Sandy came out.

That took Dylan aback. He hadn't seen Sandy

since the night he'd left him at the hospital. The young production assistant was on crutches with his leg in a full-length cast. He hobbled down the steps, and started for the set.

Sandy's face lit up when he saw Dylan. "Hey, man, how are you? I wanted to say hi, but you were working when I got here. How's it going?"

"Fine, fine," Dylan said. "How's it going with you?"

"For a guy with a broken leg, not bad. I got three more weeks in this cast, then they take it off and put on another that's slimmer, trimmer, sportier. The way they tell it, the girls will be all over me."

"What are you doing here?"

"Peter invited me. How do you like that? He knows I can't work, but he thought I'd get a kick out of seeing the filming."

"You were just talking to him?"

"He was just talking to me. He wanted to apologize for not having any time for me, what with Billy getting arrested and all."

Dylan felt a pang of guilt about pumping Sandy for information, but he had no choice. "Is Billy in there with him?"

"No, but his father is. Peter's father, Stone Barrington. He's an attorney, just came out from New York to handle the situation. He's the one who got Billy out of jail."

None of this was what Dylan wanted. "But Billy's not there?"

"Just Peter and his father. His dad was on the phone making dinner reservations at Musso and Frank. Pretty fancy, huh? Reservation for seven."

"Seven o'clock? That's pretty early when we're shooting on location."

"No, seven people. Stone flew out here with his buddy, who just happens to be, get this, the police commissioner of New York City!"

Dylan looked impressed. "Tell me more."

Dylan slipped away from Sandy and whipped out his cell phone.

"Billy Barnett is nowhere to be found, but the lawyer who bailed him out is. He happens to be Peter Barrington's father and is associated with the firm Woodman and Weld in New York. He flew out here on his private jet and brought with him as reinforcement no less than the New York City police commissioner, Dino Bacchetti. **He** is the father of Ben Bacchetti, the head of the studio. Everyone Barnett knows is a powerhouse. That accounts for how he got out of jail. But I still don't know how he managed to show up on the set and disappear."

"Then what good is any of that?" Sylvester snapped.

"Stone Barrington made a reservation for seven at Musso and Frank. I figure that's Stone Barrington, Dino Bacchetti, their sons and daughters-in-law. The seventh would be Billy Barnett. The reservation's for eight o'clock. Does that help you any?"

"We'll see."

57

Teddy got a few hours of sleep before a gofer banged on the door to summon him to Peter's trailer. Teddy pulled himself together and went over.

Stone Barrington was waiting for him.

"Sorry to drag you over here," Stone said, "but Peter figured it would be less conspicuous to summon you to his trailer than for me to call on Mark Weldon in his."

"He's right about that," Teddy said. He flopped into a chair. "This life of crime is exhausting. Anyway, what's going on?"

"Dino and I are taking everyone out to dinner. The kids and you. Think you can stay awake for it?"

"I'm sure I can. I'm not sure it's advisable to go."

Stone frowned. "Why not?"

"It seems to be open season on Billy Barnett. Everywhere he goes, people want to kill him or frame him for murder. I'm not sure spending time in his company would be conducive to your health and well-being."

"You're not coming?"

"After you came all the way from New York? Perish the thought. I certainly intend to be there, I'm just not sure Billy Barnett should."

"I see."

"On the other hand, if you chose to honor the Oscar nominees, I'll bet Mark Weldon could put in an appearance."

Stone grinned. "Works for me."

Stone raised his glass. "To **Desperation at Dawn.** May it sweep the Oscars."

The toast was met by howls of protests.

"Dad!" Peter said. "You can't say that."

Stone shrugged. "So I'm a little biased."

Hattie patted Peter on the arm. "He's a lawyer, honey. He doesn't get show business."

Everyone laughed.

"Well, I like that," Stone said. "I don't get show business."

"It's tradition, Dad. You don't jinx the show by wishing it well. You say 'break a leg.'"

Dino said, "In an effort not to bring us bad luck, I have a gang of thugs going around breaking the legs of all the other nominees."

"I'm not sure you understand the concept, Dad," Ben said.

Teddy grinned. It was fun to be among friends as Oscar-nominated actor Mark Weldon. It was as if he had no obligations and was just there to be honored.

On the other side of the restaurant Gino Patelli scowled over his cognac. "You promise me Billy Barnett, and you give me a second-rate actor."

"I didn't promise you Billy Barnett," Sylvester said. "Dylan did. And the actor's up for an Oscar."

"So's the producer. If they're having an Oscar dinner, the producer should be there."

"The guy was in jail and then spent the whole day hiding out on set. He's probably trying to avoid the press—it's not surprising he'd skip a dinner."

"With the lawyer who got him out, for Christ's sake? You'd think he'd be grateful."

"The producer's not a relation. The others are."

"The actor isn't."

"He's an Oscar nominee."

"Well, bully for him. You think I give a shit? I came here because the producer was supposed to be here." Gino scowled. "Now that I'm stuck in the goddamned restaurant, I tell you, the food better be good."

"Musso and Frank? It's famous. The food's excellent."

"We haven't got it yet."

"We just ordered," Sylvester said. He wanted to bite back the words. It was hard to know how far he could go with Gino Patelli. If he agreed with him all the time, Gino would call him on it as a yes-man. So he disagreed every now and then. Figuring out how often was a tough balancing act. "You want to cancel dinner? We can say something came up and walk out."

"We gotta eat somewhere. Maybe the guy will show up."

The food came and Gino cut into his steak. He grudgingly had to admit it was good.

At the other table, Teddy noticed Gino and Sylvester getting served. He wondered if they were dining there in search of Billy Barnett. He had a feeling they were, which opened up interesting possibilities. Had he been tailed to the restaurant? No, they might have followed Billy Barnett, but not Mark Weldon. Had they found out where Stone's party would be dining and assumed he would be part of it? Much more likely.

There was one other possibility, even more disturbing.

They had come to the restaurant not caring whether Billy Barnett showed up or not. Not able to get a line on Billy Barnett himself, Gino was checking out Billy Barnett's friends.

58

Teddy got up early the next morning and called Mike Freeman, the head of Strategic Services. Mike answered at his office in New York.

"Hey, Mike, how's it going?"

"I think I know that voice."

"I think you do, too."

"I understand congratulations are in order."

"Yes, indeed. The Oscars. Peter has every reason to be proud."

"I understand his producer and supporting actor are also being honored."

"I'm sure they're thrilled. That's not why I'm calling."

"I didn't figure it was."

"What sort of protection do you have on Peter's and Ben's families?"

"I can't give out that information."

"I know you can't. Except to the person hiring you. That happens to be me."

"Not according to my records."

"Then your records aren't up-to-date. Let's correct that while I have you on the phone. I'm hiring Strategic Services to provide protection to Peter's and Ben's families in addition to whatever protection Stone Barrington may have requested that you can't tell me about."

"You mind telling me why?"

"Circumstances have arisen which make such precautions seem prudent."

"Would this have anything to do with any recent felony arrests in the Los Angeles area?"

"That's what I don't know, and it bothers me. Clearly someone has it in for Billy Barnett. In addition to the legal entanglements, there have been personal encounters."

"Nothing you couldn't handle, I trust?"

"No, but the resultant frustration might cause the opposition to try an alternative tack. I'm afraid I might be inadvertently putting friends of mine at risk."

"This is a secure line, swept every day. Would you care to be specific?"

"I wouldn't mind, but I don't know. The evidence seems to indicate Gino Patelli's attempting to avenge his uncle's death. The fact that I didn't kill him makes it somewhat ironic."

"Any chance of bringing Patelli around to that point of view?"

"I don't think he'd be inclined to listen. And I **was** at least indirectly responsible. Anyway, I actually met the gentleman at a party, and his men tried to spoil my exit. The result no doubt added to Patelli's list of grievances."

"And that's why you're nervous."

"This was an Oscar party. Hattie's nominated for the musical score. Tessa's nominated for Best Actress. The award show is next Sunday. A vindictive creep might want to see they missed the ceremony."

"Any indication that's the case?"

"Stone took the kids out to dinner last night. Gino Patelli was in the same restaurant."

"Checking on Billy Barnett?"

"Maybe, but Billy Barnett wasn't there."

"Uh-oh."

"So, I'd like to make sure the kids are safe and well and get to the Oscars."

"If you want my men in the audience, that will take a little doing."

"That shouldn't be necessary. Just see that everyone gets there. They're fine once they're inside."

"You got it."

"I realize there may be some overlap. Don't worry about billing Stone Barrington and me for the same men. No one does what you do better than you do it. I just need to know until the Oscars there's no one I have to look out for but me."

"I take it you don't want personal protection?"

"Don't waste your men. I'd only have to ditch 'em."

Teddy hung up the phone feeling a lot better knowing Mike was on the case. He made himself up as Mark Weldon and headed for the set.

59

Viveca was touching up her makeup when she heard a knock on the trailer door. It was most likely Dylan summoning her to the set. She'd thought she had more time and was a little annoyed at the intrusion.

"Come in," she snapped.

It was Tessa. She came in hesitantly, understandable after that rude greeting. "I'm sorry to disturb you. I can come back."

Viveca flashed her hundred-watt smile and put up her hands.

"No, no, not at all. I thought they wanted me on the set, and I'm not ready to go. By all means, come on in."

"Are you sure?"

"Absolutely. Sit down while I finish my makeup. Otherwise they'll call me and I won't be ready."

Tessa sat at the kitchen table. "Isn't that the worst? I hate it when that happens."

"There's coffee in that urn. Grab a cup."

"Thanks." Tessa poured a cup, added sugar, and stirred it around. "What a week. Billy Barnett getting arrested, and all."

"I can't believe he did it."

"Of course he didn't do it. It's absurd." Tessa shook her head. "Anyway, I wanted to say I'm sorry. About the gossip columnist. Manny Rosen, wasn't it?"

Viveca frowned. "What do you mean?"

"I heard he was a friend of yours."

Viveca tensed. Did Tessa know she was behind those stories about her? Was she implying a connection?

"Not really a friend," Viveca said. "I knew him. In this business it's advisable to keep on the good side of gossip columnists if you can."

"Tell me about it. I haven't been around long enough to build up much of a network in the industry, but that's good advice. Anyway, I just wanted to say I'm sorry, and I'm here to help if there's anything I can do."

Viveca had been in the business long enough to

know that actresses could fake sincerity, but Tessa's open, honest face seemed easy to read. She really just wanted to be friends.

Though she had many acquaintances and hangers-on, Viveca had made few true friends in the business. Her longest relationship of any kind was with Bruce, whom she'd known since high school and who didn't really understand the ins and outs of Hollywood. But it seemed she might have a chance, here, to form a real bond.

"I'd actually love some company for lunch tomorrow. Should we have a commissary date?"

Tessa smiled. "I'd like that."

Across town, Bruce watched the news report with satisfaction. It couldn't have worked out better. The gossip columnist was dead, the producer had been blamed, and no one had the faintest idea he was involved.

Bruce was very proud of himself. He wished he could tell Viveca, but she wouldn't approve. Viveca was a civilian. She didn't understand combat, and this was combat whether you called it that or not. When people were out to get you, they had to be stopped. It was as simple as that. If war had taught him one thing, it was survival of the fittest. Life depended on it. The only way to survive was to beat your opponent. To outthink, outsmart, outlast him by any means possible.

The gossip columnist had posed a threat to Viveca and had to be removed, whether that was what she wanted or not. She wasn't a warrior, she was an actress. He had to make choices for her, to protect her. He had taken action, and he'd done it well.

So what if no one was going to praise him for it? It was better if nobody knew.

60

Gino Patelli was in a mood. He'd spent two and a half futile hours sitting in a restaurant waiting for Billy Barnett, and the fact that the food was excellent had done nothing for his disposition.

It didn't help when Dylan called from the set to report that Billy Barnett had not shown up again.

"I don't get it," Gino said. "Isn't the guy supposed to stay in the area?"

Sylvester smiled. "Damned if he isn't." He whipped out his cell phone and called his police informant.

. . . .

Officer Murphy stuck his head into ADA Felson's office.

"What is it, Officer?"

"You're in charge of the Billy Barnett prosecution, right? For the murder of the gossip columnist?"

At the moment Billy Barnett was only charged with a B&E, but Felson saw no reason to correct the officer. "That's right. Why?"

"He's not supposed to leave the jurisdiction of the court, is he? Because he hasn't been home, and he hasn't been at the movie studio where he works."

"Aren't they shooting a picture? I was told his presence on set was necessary."

"Yes. I was just down by the set and he isn't there, either. That's why I thought I should tell you. I can't imagine a guy like that would jump bail, unless the case against him was very bad. Anyway, I thought you'd want to know."

"Thanks, Officer. Good job."

Officer Murphy nodded and went out.

ADA Felson frowned and picked up the phone.

Teddy fished the cell phone out of his pocket and checked caller ID. It was his secretary. He pressed the button and took the call. "Yes, Margaret?"

"I just got a call from ADA Felson looking for

you. He mentioned something about not leaving
the jurisdiction of the court. I assured him you
hadn't, but he didn't seem convinced."

"That's a nuisance."

"Isn't it?"

"What does he want me to do?"

"He asked you to return his call, I have his
number."

Teddy took down the number from Margaret,
hung up, and called the ADA. "I hear you're looking for me."

"I wasn't, actually, but it's been brought to my
attention that you're nowhere to be found. You
wouldn't have left town, would you?"

"I have not. We have a deal."

"I'm afraid I require some assurance you're in
compliance with the bail arrangement."

"I assure you I am."

"While your personal assurance is nice, what I
need is a personal **appearance**. No one's seen you
since you were granted bail. You **haven't been** home,
you haven't been at work. You haven't been around
the movie set, where I was told your contribution
was vital."

"Do you take such a personal interest in all your
defendants?"

"That's why I have such a good track record. Any
reason you haven't been home?"

"I don't recall all the terms of the bail agreement, but I don't believe providing explanations for my actions was part of it. But you seem like a nice guy, so let me give you a hint. I'm a movie producer. I have a picture up for an Academy Award. I was unlucky enough to get a felony arrest. The fact that it involves a gossip columnist is like catnip for other gossip columnists. If I were living at home I'd be driving in and out through a forest of cameras and microphones, generating just the opposite type of publicity the studio is hoping to generate. Does that make sense to you?"

"Extremely reasonable," ADA Felson said. "But I'm afraid I still require proof you're not calling me from a South Seas island. When can I see you?"

"I happen to be on location now," Teddy said. "Care to drop by the set?"

"You're on location right now?"

"That's right."

"How come no one's seen you?"

"They have more important things to deal with. They're shooting a picture. If you don't believe me, come on down."

"I'd prefer you came here," ADA Felson said. "After all, you're the one getting the concessions."

"'Concessions'? Oh, you mean being charged with the **lesser** crime I didn't commit. I suppose you could call that a concession. Okay, I'll be there this afternoon."

Teddy hung up and checked the schedule. Mark Weldon wasn't due on the set for a good hour.

Teddy went to the closet and took out his makeup kit.

61

Teddy was on guard as he drove to the courthouse. The summons from ADA Felson didn't quite ring true. An ADA might want to make sure a defendant on bail hadn't left the jurisdiction of the court, but why would Felson think he had? It didn't add up, unless someone had put the idea in his head.

Someone with an ulterior motive.

Teddy spotted them from half a block away. Two goons in two black sedans were staking out the entrance to the courthouse. It was a good thing he'd driven a nondescript production car instead of something flashy and easy to spot.

The goons hadn't seen him yet. Teddy pulled

his car into a parking spot on the side of the street and surveilled his options. He was made up as Billy Barnett and didn't feel like altering his appearance just to get in the door of the courthouse.

An SCE truck was parked in the middle of the street, and a ladder had been lowered into an open manhole. As Teddy watched, the two men from the truck climbed down into the hole.

Teddy got out of his car, skirted the manhole, and hopped into the back of the truck. He was out moments later, wearing an SCE slicker and hard hat, and carrying a stack of traffic cones in front of his face. He walked around the truck and headed for the courthouse, placing a cone in the street every twenty yards or so as if cordoning off a traffic lane.

The goons in the cars never gave him a second look. Teddy worked his way across the street, slung the cones over his shoulder, and went up the steps and into the courthouse.

Once inside, he shrugged off the rain slicker, draped it over the remaining cones, and topped it off with the hard hat.

Teddy strode down the corridor, located the ADA's office, and went in the door.

ADA Felson glanced up from his desk. "Billy Barnett. So you **are** in town."

"Of course I am. I'm a law-abiding citizen. The

judge said stick around, so I stuck around. I'm insulted you thought I might do anything else."

"Despite the fact that no one's seen you since the arraignment."

"Is that a fact?"

"Yes, it is."

"According to whom?"

ADA Felson frowned. "I beg your pardon?"

"Is it standard procedure for prosecutors to keep track of defendants on bail?"

"I wasn't happy with the disposition of the arraignment. Do you know how many defendants would have walked away without some kind of murder charge? Is it any wonder I'm keeping tabs on you?"

"Bullshit. No one's keeping tabs on me. Someone tipped you off." Teddy flopped himself comfortably into a chair. "I'm not supposed to talk to you without my lawyer present, and if he were here he'd tell me to keep my mouth shut. Which is good advice, but I don't choose to take it. So let's explore a hypothetical, shall we? Someone's trying to set me up. But they can't, because they can't find me. So they come crying to you, and they get **you** to find me. Now, I'm too nice a guy to believe you might be in collusion with these people, so I'm assuming you're an unwitting dupe."

Felson flushed. "Now, look here—"

"Oh, don't start. I'm on your side. I'm actually trying to help you. If I seem rude, you might consider which one of us is trying to convict the other. The point is, if people are suggesting you check up on me, you might want to examine their motives. Not to sound immodest, but I'm an important guy in Hollywood, and nobody rises to such a lofty position without gaining a few enemies."

ADA Felson thought that over.

"So if there's nothing else, I've got to check in with my attorney." Teddy smiled. "You'll be happy to know he's leaving town."

Teddy donned the SCE gear, came out of the courthouse, and walked right by the goons waiting out front. He threw the slicker and hard hat into the back of the SCE van, hopped in the production car, and drove out to the Santa Monica Airport, where Stone had left his jet. The two men watched while the hangar pilot readied the plane.

"Try not to get arrested between now and the Oscars," Stone said.

"I'll try to see that trouble doesn't find me."

"Just stay away from the cops. I know you'd like to solve this crime, but do me a favor: don't. At least wait until after the awards. If not for your own well-being, do it for Peter. It's not every day my son gets nominated for an Oscar."

"I wouldn't do anything to jeopardize that."

"Thanks."

"But in the spirit of full disclosure, I can't let this rest. The cops have me pegged for the murder. They're not looking at anyone else, or seeking out evidence that points elsewhere. The only way we can clear my name is an independent investigation."

"If it comes to that, there are people I can hire to do those things."

"Not as well as I can. I'd hate to go to jail because your investigator didn't see something I would have."

"I don't want to argue with you. I'm advising you as your attorney. If you don't want to follow my advice, you can always hire another attorney."

"Don't be silly."

"I just want a little assurance before I get on the plane."

"Of course."

"So lay low, take it easy, and above all keep away from the cops."

"You got it."

62

Teddy hauled his bulk up the steps of the police station. He'd opted for pudgy, middle-aged patrolman Frank Johnson, an out-of-shape, over-the-hill cop just going through the motions until retirement. He lurched through the door, leaned against the watercooler, and panted a couple of times, catching his breath.

Teddy glanced over at the bullpen area, where a handful of cops labored away at desks, and said, "Who's got the video?"

A middle-aged cop looked up in annoyance. "You expect me to know what that is?"

"I don't expect anybody to know what that is. I

expect it to be a major pain in the ass that ruins my day." Teddy coughed and slumped into a chair.

"What video are you talking about?"

"Some gossip columnist got killed. They wanted video of his building, but there wasn't any."

"Then you can't get it."

"No shit. So now they want video of the whole block, to see if the suspect's on it. So that's my shit job for today. See if I can spot the guy walking toward the apartment."

"What's wrong with that?"

"They don't need to prove the guy was walking **toward** the apartment. They arrested the guy **in** the apartment. What does it **matter** if he was seen walking toward the apartment?"

"Maybe they want to prove how long he was there," a young cop suggested.

"Whoa, look at the rookie cop, sticking up for his fellow officers, trying to justify the shit work they passed on to me."

"I been a cop for ten years."

"That's a rookie to me. Do me a favor, will you? Point me in the direction of whoever can show me the video so I don't have a heart attack going up and down stairs."

A half hour later Teddy was ensconced in a little cubicle with a laptop computer and thumb drives of surveillance video. He let the young cop show him how to use them, though he could have taught the kid a thing or two. Then he settled in to search.

The problem was not having an accurate time of death. The police weren't going to release one, not having arrested him in the apartment. The prosecutor would want the time of death to be as close to that as possible. Any evidence contradicting that theory would be quickly suppressed.

Teddy's impression had been that the body hadn't been dead long, but whether that meant a half hour or two and a half was hard to ascertain without a careful inspection. The cops' arrival had been unfortunate on so many levels. Not getting an accurate TOD was the least of it.

Teddy looked at the video from the cameras that were closest to the decedent's apartment building on the same side of the street. He found one that was focused on the building two doors down to the east, and another focused on the building two doors down to the west.

He picked one randomly, punched in about an hour before his arrest, and ran the video forward, looking for anyone headed in the direction of the apartment. Several people went by, but no one he recognized. That didn't mean he hadn't seen the killer, but it was a fairly good indication. Gino Patelli was out to get him and would have sent one of his closest enforcers. No one he had seen fit the part.

Teddy sped through an hour's worth of video from the other direction. Once again, he saw nothing helpful.

Teddy went back to the first video and started it two hours before his arrest. As the images danced across the screen, he suddenly blinked and took his finger off the fast-forward button. He rewound slightly.

Yes, it was someone he knew, but from where?

His mouth fell open.

The odd young man he'd met at the party, Viveca Rothschild's boyfriend. So, he was walking in the gossip columnist's neighborhood not long before the crime. Could he be protecting his girlfriend? The gossip columnist wasn't writing about her, but he **was** writing about her costar in the movie she was filming.

It wasn't much, but it was the only thing he had so far.

Teddy ran the video the rest of the hour to see if there was anyone else of interest on the tape. There wasn't.

The boyfriend was the lead. He had walked down the street toward the apartment. But had he gone inside?

That was a little harder to verify. Teddy took

out the thumb drive and stuck in the other one. He watched the video from the camera to the west.

Sure enough, halfway through the video, here came the young man. Teddy was frustrated. The guy had just been walking down the street, out of the frame of one camera and into the frame of the next moments later.

Or **was** it moments later?

What was the time on the tape?

Teddy checked the time stamp. Viveca's boyfriend was walking away from the apartment at 3:45. What time was he walking toward it in the other video?

Teddy stuck in the thumb drive and rewound the tape. And here he came down the street at . . . ? 3:32.

He was walking at a normal clip. The second camera should have picked him up within one minute. But the gap was nearly thirteen minutes long.

There was room for discrepancy. But thirteen minutes? That was a hell of a disparity.

Teddy rewatched the footage more closely, looking for any further clues. He ran it slow, backed it up, ran it again. Not that much to see. Just the young man walking right along. His arms were swinging freely.

Except.

Teddy froze the image. He ran it back and forth.

The young man flexed the fingers of his right hand. He straightened them out, retracted them into a fist, then relaxed them again. It was momentary, but it was there. Just the sort of thing a fighter would do if he hurt his hand throwing a punch.

Or stabbing someone in the heart.

63

Teddy drove to the set and changed back into Mark Weldon. It was fifteen minutes till his call. Not as much time as he'd have liked, but still it was better than nothing.

Teddy hurried up the steps of Viveca's trailer and pushed the door open. In his haste, he'd forgotten to knock.

Viveca glanced up from her makeup table. "Why, Mr. Weldon," she said, batting her eyes. "How impetuous of you."

Teddy grinned. "You've done drawing-room comedy."

"I was Gwendolen in **The Importance of Being**

Earnest and Lydia Languish in **The Rivals**. I wasn't always a femme fatale."

"And yet you're so good at it."

"Why, Mr. Weldon. Are you flirting with me?"

"Not likely. I saw that slab of beef you brought to Robert Vincent's Oscar party. I wouldn't want to tangle with him."

"No kidding. You may be tough on-screen, but he's the real deal."

"How come he's not watching the filming?"

"My image. My publicist doesn't want me to have a boyfriend hanging around the set. It increases my appeal to the male audience if I appear to be available."

"But it's okay at the party?"

"Someone has to accompany me. It's a bit different than a jealous boyfriend mooning around the set."

"Is he jealous?"

"That's how the publicist paints it. I tell you, I'm lucky to have a life."

There was a knock on the door and Dylan stuck his head in. "Oh. Sorry, Miss Rothschild. I didn't know you had company."

"It's all right. Did you need something?"

"Just wanted to see if there was anything you wanted."

"They didn't send for me?"

"No."

"Then I'm all set. Thanks, Dylan."

He nodded and went out, closing the door.

"See?" Viveca said. "That's all it takes. By lunchtime it will be all over the set that you and I are having an affair."

"And if I weren't here, it would be all over the set that you were having an affair with Dylan," Teddy said with a smile.

"He is cute, isn't he?"

"Not my type," Teddy said.

"Am I your type?"

"You're everyone's type. That's what makes you a star. Every man in the theater wants to be with you, and probably half the women."

Viveca chuckled. "So, what did you want?"

"Oh, I like what you're doing. In the scene, I mean. It's coming across more and more that while I may be in charge, you're actually calling the shots. I just wanted to say, it's perfect, don't change a thing."

Viveca looked at him. "You're not the average actor."

"Hey, I'm a stuntman who got lucky. I'm happy just to be here. And I admire your talent in the scene. I just wanted to tell you I appreciate it."

"Thanks."

"Is that guy really your boyfriend?"

"Dylan?"

"No, not Dylan. The ex-military type from the party."

"I know he seems intimidating, but he's really very sweet."

"You're not going to give me a straight answer?"

"And piss off my publicist?"

"That's what I thought," Teddy said. He smiled. "Well, I can understand your publicist being nervous. This certainly is a snakebit production. Tessa getting all that bad press, just when she should be coasting on the Oscars publicity and the news of the two of you starring together in this picture. We don't need stories of you hiding a secret boyfriend. There's only so much gossip one film can take."

"No kidding."

"See you on the set."

Teddy went out the door not having learned much. The only telling phrase was "jealous boyfriend." It was something to be considered. A jealous ex-serviceman relegated to the sidelines while his girlfriend's star was on the rise could harbor resentment.

Teddy wondered what the young man thought of all this.

64

Viveca got home, mixed herself a martini, and flopped onto a deck chair on the veranda.

Bruce padded out in a bathing suit and T-shirt. He looked happy. Viveca felt horribly conflicted, what with Manny getting killed, and her producer a prime suspect. Had Billy Barnett done it, to stop him from spreading lies about Tessa? If he had, it was all her fault.

Damn the Oscars. If the award hadn't pitted Tessa against her, everything would be fine. Manny would be alive, and Viveca would be swept up in filming her exciting new picture.

Then Viveca realized that no, she wouldn't. She'd only taken the part in the film in order to undermine Tessa. Now that they'd become friends, her plans had all gone to hell. And yet . . . the lure of the Oscar was still undeniable. The recognition, the respect. If she were honest with herself, Viveca knew she'd be devastated to lose, even to a friend.

"'S'matter?" Bruce said. It was one of his favorite contractions. Viveca usually found it cute. Now it just irritated her.

She didn't know what to tell him. Certainly not the truth. Bruce had enough trouble with straightforward concepts, but her convoluted mixed feelings were beyond his scope.

"Just worried about the Oscars."

Bruce flopped down in a deck chair. "You're going to win."

"I might win."

"You will. You were great."

"Tessa was great, too."

"Tessa was okay."

"You saw the movie?"

"Everyone saw the movie."

Viveca frowned. It was the wrong thing to say, but Bruce didn't know he was being unconsciously gauche.

"She won't win," he said.

Lately it was his go-to answer for everything. He didn't realize how grating it was for her to hear it.

"If she wins, she wins. I don't mean to be a poor

sport. I just can't stand the idea of sitting there, keeping a smile on my face for the cameras while I listen to her acceptance speech."

"You won't have to."

"Why not?"

"I'll stop her."

"How?"

"I'll run up the steps and tackle her."

Viveca smiled at the thought. She shook her head. "No, you won't."

"Yes, I will. And that's all they'll write about. How the wrong person got the award."

"You're not going to do that." Viveca looked Bruce in the eyes.

"Yes, I am."

Viveca took a breath. "Promise me you're not going to do that."

That caught him up short. **Promise me** was Viveca's safe word, the line he could not cross. When she asked him to promise her something, he knew better than to break that promise.

"I promise. I won't do that."

"Good."

"But she's not making that speech, I promise you that."

Viveca smiled. That was also Bruce's MO. When she made him promise something, he always promised something else he would do instead. Usually nothing came of it. She did what she always did, accepted his promise without argument and moved on, hoping it would be quickly forgotten.

Viveca's martini was empty. She smiled at Bruce, got up from the deck chair, and went to make herself another.

Bruce leaned back in his deck chair and thought. This time he had not made an idle declaration. He had a very definite goal in mind, one that was in keeping with his military training and would allow him to keep his promise to Viveca.

If she won, Tessa would not be giving her speech.

Smiling, Bruce heaved himself out of the deck chair and dove into the pool.

He swam laps, and laid his plans.

65

Teddy called Strategic Services. "Hi, Mike, any news?"

"None."

"No one's made a move on the protectees?"

"Not at all. From the reports I got, no one's paying the least attention to any of them."

"Glad to hear it."

"Do you want me to ease back on the coverage?"

"Not at all. Your report is the best news I've had in a long time. You've made my day."

"Our best work is when we do nothing."

"Damned if it isn't. Keep at it until the Oscars."

Teddy hung up the phone. He couldn't help

feeling uneasy. It was the old cliché: "It's quiet. Too quiet." The thing was, no one was bothering him, either. Granted, no one could find him. Still, it didn't seem like anyone was looking.

What was Gino Patelli up to?

66

ouldn't he have come to us?" Gino Patelli said.

It was not the first time he had said it. Gino and Sylvester were making their way up the narrow dirt road of the Royal Academy Long-Distance Rifle Range. The name of the place was misleading. The range had nothing to do with anything royal, and was not affiliated with any academy. It was merely a place up in the hills where gun enthusiasts could discharge high-powered rifles without the danger of shooting up a pool party a quarter of a mile away.

"Why can't we drive in?"

"It disturbs the shooters. The tiniest vibration gets magnified a thousand times at that distance."

"I don't see why he can't come to us."

"He wants to make sure you'll hire him."

"Why wouldn't I hire him?"

"He doesn't interview well. He lets his gun do the talking."

There came the sound of shots up ahead.

"These people do know which way they're aiming?" Gino said.

They started passing shooting stations. They were separated from each other and camouflaged like duck blinds, though presumably they were shooting at nothing but targets. There were tripods mounted in the stations should someone wish to use one, stanchions to lean against, and mats on the ground should a shooter wish to fire from the prone position.

All of the shooting stations were in use. Most shooters were using tripods.

At one station a man lay facedown on the mat, his head cradled in his arms. To all appearances, he was sound asleep. "You lookin' for me?" he said. He had not raised his head.

"Depends who you are," Sylvester said.

"We spoke on the phone."

"How do you know that?"

"Please." The man rolled over and sat up. He was a wiry man in battle fatigues with unkempt black hair and an unshaven face. "Okay. I'm who you think I am. You're who I think you are. Do you want my services?"

Gino wasn't sure he did. The man's manner was hostile, his eyes cold and threatening. A man accustomed to a degree of deference, Gino was tempted to tell the guy to go fuck himself. What stopped him was the fact that perhaps the situation called for such a man.

"Can you hit a moving target?"

"Are you stupid?"

Gino blinked. "Fuck you," he said, and turned to go.

"Hold on," Sylvester said. "The man meant no offense. He's just explaining how it is, aren't you?"

"No one's ever hired me to shoot a stationary target. If the target's stationary, the job's over."

"And you brought us up here to show us how good you are?" Gino said.

"I'd like to. My sight is slightly off. I need to recalibrate."

"So, recalibrate."

"Not now. In my workshop."

"You brought me all the way up here and you're going to miss?"

"I'm not going to miss. I'll be a few millimeters left of dead center." The man picked up a pair of binoculars and handed them to Gino. "Check out the target."

Gino looked. "That seems pretty close."

"Not **that** target. Up the hill to the right. Let me know when you find it."

Gino scanned the distance. He spotted it. "You can hit that?"

A shot rang out.

Gino flinched and turned around.

The man was just lowering his rifle. He shook his head. "Left of center."

Gino lifted the binoculars to his eyes to verify, then looked the man over. "Let's talk business."

Two hundred fifty thousand. Half up front."

"You have got to be kidding."

"Why would I kid about a thing like that?"

"That's an insane amount of money."

"Are you calling me insane?"

"Of course not. I'm saying that is way more than I would normally pay."

"Then you should hire the guys you would normally pay. Maybe this time they'll have better luck."

Gino considered that. He took a breath.

"What's your name?"

"None of your business."

"If I pay you two hundred and fifty thousand dollars, it's my business."

"I'm the shooter. That's all you need to know."

"You want me to call you the shooter?"

"I don't give a damn what you call me as long as you pay me."

"What do I get for two hundred and fifty thousand dollars?"

"I will hit the target."

"You never miss?"

"This conversation is boring me. I only take the jobs I want. I'm not sure I want yours. Who is the target?"

Gino nodded to Sylvester.

Sylvester reached into a large manila envelope and handed him a glossy photograph.

The shooter looked at it. "Who is this?"

"Billy Barnett."

"Why have I heard that name?"

"He was arrested recently as a suspect in the death of a gossip columnist."

"He's in jail?"

"He's out on bail."

"What's the problem?"

"Since he got out of jail, he hasn't shown up at home or at the movie set."

"You're telling me you don't know where the target is?"

"Not at the present time. He has to be found. But isn't that what you do?"

"No, that's what a private investigator does. If you want me to do that as well as the shooting, it will cost you three hundred thousand."

Before Gino could explode, Sylvester jumped in. "We don't know where he is, but we know where he will be."

"Oh?"

"His picture's been nominated for an Academy Award. The Oscars ceremony is Sunday night."

"You want me to kill him on national TV?" the shooter asked, appearing intrigued by the challenge.

Gino nearly gagged.

"You're not going to kill him on camera," Sylvester said. "The event will be televised. We're simply advising you about where and when you can locate the target."

"Fine. But how do I pick him out in a crowd full of guys in penguin suits?"

Gino and Sylvester had hoped the photograph would be sufficient, but the man was right—at formal events, men in tuxes tended to all blend together. Gino gave Sylvester a meaningful look.

Sylvester said, "We will find his seat location and communicate it to you before the event concludes." He didn't know yet how they'd accomplish **that** herculean task, but it wouldn't matter if they couldn't get the shooter onboard. "If all else fails, you will have seen him in person and can more easily ID him the next time we have a credible location."

The man considered for a moment, then gave a curt nod, which Gino and Sylvester took to be a seal on their agreement. Then he smiled at Sylvester. "And one last thing: I'll need access to the area. You will have to get me a ticket."

67

Bruce parked his car at a meter and walked down the street to Maury's Bar. It was, as usual, crowded and dimly lit, the noise coming from an old-fashioned jukebox playing actual 45s.

Maury's catered to veterans. Soldiers drank half-price drafts, not just during happy hour, but right up until closing. It particularly catered to wounded vets. Purple Hearts got dollar drafts, and usually someone else would buy them.

PFC Jasper White was drinking for free at the end of the bar. Jasper wasn't from his unit; Bruce had met him in the VA hospital. Jasper had a scar down the side of his face as a result of an explosion that caught him when a wayward rocket hit a munitions dump. The resultant traumatic brain injury sent Jasper home.

Bruce slid in next to him. "Fire in the hole."

Jasper looked up and smiled. "Hey, D-man. How's it going?" Jasper and Bruce were both demolition experts. Jasper referred to them as D-men. "What you drinkin'?"

"What you buyin'?"

"Me?" Jasper said. "You're the one with the fancy girlfriend."

"All right, what am **I** buying?"

"She's really your girlfriend?"

"She's really my girlfriend."

Bruce and Jasper had this conversation every time they got together. Jasper could never believe the blonde goddess up on the screen was actually with Bruce. After all, Jasper had never seen the two of them together. It seemed like a tall tale. Something one soldier brags about to another.

"How come you're not in any of the pictures?"

"I'm not an actor."

Jasper waved it away. "I don't mean in the movies. I mean in the magazines. The newspapers. There was that spread in **People** magazine. I didn't see you."

"They want her to be a sex symbol, like Marilyn Monroe. They think a steady boyfriend ruins the image."

"Oh, go on."

"They had meetings about it. Would it be good for her image to be dating a vet?"

"Wouldn't it?"

"Better to be single."

"Even a wounded vet?"

"Wounded wouldn't cut it. For her to acknowledge me, I'd have to be killed in action."

"Get out of here."

Bruce signaled the bartender and ordered two more drafts.

Jasper's PTSD was far worse than Bruce's.

"So, do you miss it?" Bruce said.

"Miss what?"

"You know."

"Being shot at and treated like shit? Not really."

"That's the bad part."

"What's the good part?"

"You know what I mean. Blowing shit up."

Jasper looked at him. "Do you miss it?"

"Not enough to go back. But I was good at it. I liked that I was good at it, and that people counted on me. But, basically, I just like doing it. I like the thrill of seeing it go off. Nothing like it."

"Amen, brother."

"Yeah." Bruce shook his head wistfully. "I'd give anything for that rush."

Jasper drained his beer. He set the mug down on the counter and looked at Bruce.

"Got a car?"

Bruce turned down the side road. The sign read: NO THROUGH TRAFFIC.

"Isn't the dump closed this time of night?"

"To civilians," Jasper said.

"You can get in?"

"Please. You were in Iraq. You have to ask me that?"

"In Iraq you didn't get in trouble for doing what we do. You were supposed to do it."

"Hey, they taught us to blow things up. Did they really expect us to stop?"

They reached the town dump. As expected, the iron gate was closed and padlocked shut. Beyond it, in the background, Bruce could see the outlines of abandoned cars silhouetted against the night sky.

"Turn right," Jasper said.

"There's no road."

"Wimp." Jasper laughed

Bruce swung the car to the right and followed the steel mesh fence around. He prayed he wouldn't drive over a jagged piece of metal or scrape the underside of the gas tank on some unseen rock. He gritted his teeth and guided the car along.

"Stop," Jasper said.

Bruce was happy to comply.

Jasper hopped out of the car. "Pop the trunk."

On the way to the junkyard they had stopped by Jasper's apartment. He had run in and come back toting a canvas duffel bag. He pulled it out of the trunk, slung it over his shoulder. "Come on," he said, and walked up to the fence.

He flopped the duffel on the ground, unzipped it, and took out a pair of heavy-duty wire cutters. He used them to cut a four-foot slit up the side of the fence. He folded it back like a flap.

"Think you could fit through that?"

"Just watch me," Bruce said. He got down on his hands and knees and wriggled through the fence on his stomach.

He was getting filthy. He'd have to tell Viveca he got into a bar fight. She wouldn't like that.

Jasper passed him the canvas duffel and wriggled through himself.

"All right," Jasper said. "Choose your poison. I'd say a car, but it's too much to hope for gas in the tank, and you'd want a secondary explosion. A microwave is surprisingly satisfying. You hear bits of it flying everywhere, like shrapnel."

"What would you recommend?"

"I don't know." Jasper pulled a flashlight out of the duffel and switched it on. "Let's see what we've got here. Oh, wow! Look at this. Half a Mini Cooper. Imagine what the driver looked like. The bumper's in the front seat. But the passenger side is nearly intact. I bet we can blow that fucker off the ground."

"Hell, yes," Bruce said. "What are we going to use?"

Jasper reached into the duffel bag and pulled out a brick of plastic explosive. "An old favorite. C-four. Just like the good old days."

"Where did you get it?"

"Homemade, my friend," he said. Bruce had heard rumors that Jasper had access to explosives, but hadn't realized the guy made his own. He hoped to hell it was as stable as the professionally manufactured stuff.

"All right, how many bricks you think?"

"It's a Mini Cooper. One."

Jasper grabbed two bricks, leaned in the door, and reached down beneath the seat. "We only get one shot, right? Might as well make sure it counts." He positioned the plastic explosive, and straightened up. "That'll do it. Give me a blasting cap."

Bruce fumbled in the duffel and came out with a detonator. "Here you go."

Jasper reached under the seat and embedded it

into the plastic explosive. He took out a penlight and checked his work.

Apparently satisfied, Jasper led Bruce back through the fence. He stopped long enough to weave the flap closed with metal wire—a rudimentary patch, but better than a gaping hole.

"Gotta love a remote-control detonator. Don't have to jury-rig something with a fuse, light it, and run like hell."

"I've been there," Bruce said.

"Turn the car around and leave it idling and ready to go. We'll be gone before anyone reports the blast."

Bruce turned the car and got out with the door still open.

"Okay, here goes nothing," Jasper said. He pressed a button on his cell phone.

The noise was impressive. The blast was less so. There was no gas in the tank, so no secondary explosion. The little car flew to pieces, but it was hard to see.

"Hit it, hotshot!" Jasper said.

Bruce took off down the road.

He couldn't wait to get home and check out the prize he'd appropriated while Jasper rigged the bomb.

Two slabs of C-4 and a detonator.

68

Bruce drove down to the VFW looking for Frank, a stocky electrical contractor, who he found hanging out shooting the shit with the powers that be. They appeared to be planning a talent show. That was one activity Bruce had no interest in. His talent was blowing things up.

Bruce managed to lure Frank away from the group. "I was hoping you could do me a favor," he said.

"How's that?"

"I got a job."

"That you need help with?"

"Actually, no. It's an electrical job, the type you do, but it's a small job, so I don't need an assistant. Just half a day's work for a hundred and fifty bucks."

"You should get more."

"I'm happy to get anything."

"I thought you had that fancy actress taking care of you."

"I need some money she doesn't give me. Actually, I need some money she doesn't **know** about."

"You got a girl on the side? You're dating a famous actress, and you've got a girl on the side?"

Bruce felt like his head was coming off. This was just the sort of thing that triggered his PTSD. He was trying to have a simple conversation, but the guy wouldn't shut up and let him get to the point. Bruce could feel a migraine coming on.

"Anyway, the secretary wants me to do the job, but her boss is a pain in the ass, and I gotta show credentials to get in her office."

"I can't loan you my credentials."

"Of course not. But I bet you got some old work permit you could photocopy that I could white out and fill in. The guy won't know what he's looking at. He's just gotta see something, to prove to himself he's hot shit."

Frank cocked his head. "That I could do."

. . . .

The production assistant frowned. "Inspection?"

"That's right."

"I don't understand."

That was not surprising. Rachael Quigly was the fifth person Bruce had been handed off to since he'd shown up to inspect the Grande Palladium Theater.

Rachael looked at Bruce skeptically. He'd said he was a supervisor, but he looked more like a longshoreman in charge of unloading boxes down by the dock. "Why are we being inspected?"

"The Oscars weren't here last year, so everything has to be checked out. I'm mostly concerned with the stage. You're going to have hundreds of performers. That's a huge insurance risk."

"I'm sure we have adequate insurance."

Bruce had practiced what to say. "It's only valid if your inspections are up-to-date."

Rachael didn't know about that. She was from the production department, and knew more about the TV show than the theater. "Uh-huh. So what do you want to see?"

"Let's start with dessert," Bruce said. It was one of his favorite expressions, suitable for almost any occasion.

"What?" Rachael said.

"Let's see the stage."

The theater was cavernous, a vast array of seats fanning out from a deep and wide stage fronted by steps spanning the entire width, allowing easy access for the actors in the audience.

Workers of various types were going over the auditorium, cleaning and checking and making notes. An angular man with a tool belt was at the back of the stage on a ladder.

"Oh, look, there's Eddie," Rachael said. She sounded like she'd been thrown a lifeline, spotting someone she knew. "He's the head electrician. He can help you out. Hey, Eddie!"

Bruce pointed at her. "Don't go anywhere. He won't know what I want."

The electrician came over.

Rachael, desperately trying to maneuver the handoff, said, "Eddie. This is the electrical inspector, checking out the circuits. Surely you can tell him what he needs to know?"

Eddie reacted as if Bruce had invaded enemy turf. His greeting could not have been less welcoming. "Who sent you?"

"Wozniak," Bruce said. It was his go-to name. Nobody wanted to admit they didn't know Wozniak. "Said I'd have a clear field."

"Is that right?" Eddie said.

"Listen, I don't want to keep you from what you're doing. I know you're under time pressure.

Rachael can show me what I need. I'll just ask you if I have a question."

"Right," Eddie said. He couldn't get away from Bruce quick enough.

Bruce turned back to the unfortunate Rachael. "So, I'm mostly concerned with the production. You'll be having dance numbers?"

"There are five Oscar-nominated songs. Three of them have dance numbers. There's also the opening number. It starts on film, then through movie magic appears to finish up in the theater, and leaves the host onstage for the opening monologue."

"Where is that?"

"On the podium."

"In the center?"

"No. It's upstage left."

"There?"

"No. Stage left is the actor's left. It's to your right as you face the stage."

"Where do they give out the awards?"

"Downstage center."

"Exactly where?"

"Why?"

"There will be a mic there. You say that's downstage center?"

"Actually, there will be two of them. One right of center, one left of center. They'll alternate presenting from side to side."

"I'll need those spots marked off. And I'll need to know which awards are given from which."

"Why?"

"Do they tell me? They say find out. I'm sure you can get me a list. And I'll need to see where those mics line up under the stage."

"Oh." Rachael's spirits were sinking. "Really?"

"By now you got your show mapped out. Where the host is, where the presenters are, where the numbers are staged. You got a copy of that with you?"

"No."

"Well, let's get one. Where would that be, back at the office?"

"That's right. I'll go get it."

"Don't be silly. Call them. Have someone run it over."

Rachael liked the idea. She took out her cell phone, made the request. Minutes later an intern arrived with the chart. Rachael, who couldn't have been much more than an intern herself, was gratified to accept it.

"Here, let's see that," Bruce said.

He took it from her, sat on the steps, and unfolded it onto the stage.

From a distance the stage had appeared solid, but up close it was a checkerboard of cracks and lines.

"What are all the grooves in the floor?"

"Oh. Trapdoors. Removable sections. The whole

stage is trapped. You can take out any section and have an entrance from anywhere for a production number."

"What's down below?"

"Removable grids and catwalks. We've been told that there's nothing we could do at the other theater that we can't do at this one."

"Well, let's see," Bruce said, lining things up. "The spots for the presentations are here and here. And look. We have outlets sunk into the floor of the stage in both places. I'll have to check them out from below and see how they're wired. You say there's a grid down there?"

"Scaffolding and catwalks. Do you need to see?"

"Yes, I do."

Rachael led Bruce into the wings, through a fire door, and down a long stairway to the lower level.

At the bottom of the stairs they emerged into a large open area with chairs and couches scattered about.

"This is the greenroom," Rachael said, "where the actors from the show hang out. It's right below the orchestra pit. The dressing rooms are off that way, under the audience. The section you're concerned with is over here."

Directly beneath the stage, a concrete floor held scaffolding rising all the way up to the catwalks twenty-five feet above.

"The actors have to come from down here?" Bruce said.

"No, there's access to the catwalk from the wings on either side so they don't have to climb."

"We couldn't have done that?" Bruce said.

Rachael was flustered. "I thought you wanted to see it from down here."

"Not a problem."

Bruce climbed a set of metal steps up to the catwalk along the back wall of the theater. He had to stoop down to walk under the stage. He followed a maze of ramps in the direction he thought the presenters' marks might be. He could see the power lines from the outlets tacked along the support beams that held up the sections of the stage. There were many more outlets than the two he was concerned with.

Bruce maneuvered himself into position below his best guess for the stage-right presentation outlet. The stage floor next to it had a hinged trapdoor held in place by sliding wooden beams. Bruce pulled them out. The trapdoor swung down and hung on its hinges.

Bruce stuck his head through the trap and checked out the stage floor. Sure enough, the outlet he had lined up was the one he had located from the floor plan, the one where the stage-right presenter's microphone would be.

Bruce pushed the trap back up and secured it. He fished a Magic Marker out of his pocket and unobtrusively marked an X next to the bottom of that outlet.

He located the stage-left outlet in a similar manner and marked it, too.

Bruce spent another ten minutes inspecting the grid, then joined the assistant down below. He toured the rest of the theater so she wouldn't be suspicious, and let her go.

"Well, that's it," he said. Rachael was tremendously relieved, but her heart immediately sank. "I'll have to check it out one more time on the day of the show. Nothing extensive, just a quick check to make sure everything is in place. Won't take more than fifteen minutes, tops. You'll need to meet me and let me in. If everything goes smoothly, I will be able to give you a very nice boost with the boss."

Bruce favored her with a smile, and left.

It should work just fine.

69

Sherry Day was over the moon. Sleeping with that producer had been worthwhile after all. She hadn't gotten the part, but she had wound up with seats at the Oscar Awards, the hottest ticket in town. She would go dressed to the nines in a backless gown, something plunging to the waist, her outfit just screaming for attention. One way or another she would get on TV, and it would lead to something big.

She knew it was a pipe dream, but it was a nice pipe dream, and it made up for a bunch of bad readings and missed auditions and cattle-call extra work, and the whole sad cycle of desperation and despair. For one glorious night she'd be somebody.

Her cell phone rang. She fumbled for it in her purse, saying the same little prayer she always did on these occasions. "Let it be my agent."

"Sherry Day?"

"Yes?"

"My name is Sylvester, I'm a friend of Nelson Hogue's. Do you remember the party at the Richter estate?"

Sherry did. She'd begged a massive favor from Nelson, to secure her an invitation to a party at the home of a prestigious Hollywood agent. The agent didn't seem the least bit interested in her, and some of the guests got the impression she'd been hired from an escort service.

"Well, you owe him, and he owes me. I need a favor. He offered to transfer the indebtedness. I understand you're going to the Oscars."

Sherry's heart sank. "Yes, I am."

"Well, good for you. It's almost impossible to get those tickets. I'm sure you'll have a wonderful time."

Sherry's relief was palpable. "Yes, I'm sure I will."

"You have two tickets, don't you? Who is your date?"

"My boyfriend."

"Yeah. About that. I'm afraid he won't be able to go."

"What?"

"Don't worry. I have someone to take his place."

70

Peter called Teddy into his trailer between takes.

"You had something you wanted to discuss?" Teddy said.

"Oscar night. We have to work out the logistics."

"Ah, yes. You have it figured out yet?"

"To the extent that I can. For reasons that defy understanding, the awards are being held at the Grande Palladium Theater this year, instead of the usual venue. Which is a pain, because you can't get a sense of where everything is by watching previous Oscars ceremonies."

"I'm sure it will be the same."

"Some things never change. Celebrities will be

walking the red carpet for the pre-Oscar show. You and Tessa will have to do that."

"Oh, hell."

"You'll be fine. Most of the questions will be aimed at Tessa. I'd appreciate it if you'd jump in if anyone is giving her a hard time."

"I'm going to be with Tessa?"

"Yes. I've ordered the two of you a limo. It will drop you off right on the red carpet. Hattie, Ben, and I will go in quietly together. Not a recognizable face in the lot of us. We can walk in practically unscathed."

"You're an Oscar-nominated director. An interview wouldn't kill you."

Peter grinned. "That doesn't mean I have to do one. Anyway, Ben and Tessa are coming over for drinks beforehand. I figured you'd join us and we'd all leave from there."

"What time?"

"Around three. I suggested earlier, and the girls howled. Apparently there's something about dressing for these occasions that requires half the day."

"Yeah, the gowns get more ink than the awards. Luckily, a tux always looks like a tux."

"You're wearing a tux?"

"Absolutely. I'll have to be two people. I don't have to change if they're both wearing a tux."

"Good point."

"The order of the awards works for us. The first one given is always Best Supporting Actor. The presenter will read the nominees. The camera will cut to me sitting with Tessa. That will establish that Mark Weldon is there and is in the audience.

"Best Picture is the last award. So, about halfway through the show Mark Weldon will get up and go to the bathroom. Sometime after that, producer Billy Barnett will come in and take his place with you, Hattie, and Ben."

"That's fine in theory," Peter said.

"What do you mean, 'in theory'?"

"Well, in your little scenario, you're in the audience sitting next to Tessa after your category's called."

"Yeah. So?"

"Well, what happens if you win? You've got to accept the award, and even after that you can't go back down the steps into the audience. Don't they spirit you off somewhere and shoot footage of you and do backstage interviews and all that?"

"I hadn't thought of that."

"Well, think of it now. What happens if you win?"

Teddy considered. "Well, I don't think we'll have to worry."

"Why not?"

"Hell will have frozen over."

71

Teddy, in his Mark Weldon guise, took Tessa and Viveca out to a restaurant on the lunch break. They had Dylan, the production assistant, drive them. He was rapidly becoming the actors' go-to PA. At least Viveca's. She seemed to take a keen interest in the boy.

"Too bad Dylan can't come in," Viveca said, once they were seated at a table in the restaurant. Dylan, of course, remained outside in the car.

"He's got to guard the production car," Teddy said. "If anything happens to it, the production manager would have his head."

"So why'd you want to come here?" Tessa said, changing the subject.

"Oh, I just wanted to have lunch with my two best girls outside the watchful eye of the whole damn crew. It always feels like we're under a microscope on the set. It's nice to be alone."

"I hate to spoil your fun," Viveca said, "but if you glance around, heads are turning."

"Maybe so, but nobody's going to rush up and put makeup on our faces, or lead us back to a trailer for a costume change, or walk us in front of a camera to show us our marks."

No one bothered them. They ate lunch without incident.

When they were done, Viveca got a doggie bag and brought half of her beef brisket sandwich out to Dylan in the car. He munched on it gratefully as he pulled out of the parking space. The boy was clearly hungry.

"If he drives off the road it's your fault," Tessa said.

"Sorry," Dylan said. "I shouldn't be eating in the car."

"No one cares," Viveca said. "Just don't hit any large trucks and we'll be fine."

Teddy wasn't listening. He was glancing out the windows to see if anyone was taking an interest in them. He spotted two cars belonging to Mike Freeman's men, who were protecting Tessa as they'd been assigned to do. That was good to know.

It only took Teddy a few blocks to ascertain that no one else was paying any attention to the car. That was the true reason he'd taken Tessa and Viveca out to lunch. Mike Freeman's men would have reported any suspicious activity if they'd spotted it, but Teddy didn't want to rely on that alone. He wanted to see for himself.

Mike Freeman's men were good.

But he was better.

72

Gino Patelli was nervous. The one key piece of information they needed to provide to their shooter—Billy Barnett's seat location at the Oscars—still eluded them, despite all of Sylvester's connections.

"Don't we know one damn person who can find the info?"

"No," Sylvester said. It wasn't good to say no to Gino Patelli, but this was a case where the best course of action was ripping off the Band-Aid. He immediately plunged into an explanation. "The producers don't share the seat numbers of the celebrities with the ushers or staff until the last minute.

Such information is likely to slip out and makes it too easy for fans to stalk them. They don't want people pestered and made to feel uncomfortable. Their faces are going to be seen on TV. It's important that they seem to be enjoying themselves."

"That's the party line?"

"It is."

"You buy that bullshit?"

"I do. We know approximately where he's going to be sitting. Up front with the other nominees."

"This is a nightmare. If we can't give the shooter Billy Barnett's seat number, how is he going to find him?"

"The man's a professional. I'm sure he can find his target."

"I don't want **your** assurance. I want **his** assurance. And I can't fucking get it, because I can't fucking talk to him."

"I'll take care of it."

"How will you take care of it?"

"I don't know, but I will."

"Not good enough. Tell me now."

Sylvester felt uneasy. He'd had an idea, but it was a last resort that involved bringing yet another risk factor into the operation. But Gino was beginning to panic, and beggars couldn't be choosers. "The kid can do it."

"What kid?"

"Dylan. He can get Billy Barnett's seat number, and give it to the shooter."

"You think he'll be able to come through?"

"He doesn't have a choice."

"Make it work."

73

Dylan had a sick feeling in his stomach as he knocked on the door to Viveca's trailer. He'd done everything he could think of to find out where Billy Barnett would be sitting the night of the Oscars—scanned incoming mail, tried to break into Barnett's trailer, prodded Barnett's secretary until she became noticeably suspicious and clammed up. This was his last chance, his Hail Mary.

Viveca called, "Come in."

He went in and found her lying on the bed. She had taken her costume off, and was wearing a bra and panties and a skimpy makeup robe. She hadn't bothered to pull it around her. She was, as usual, completely unselfconscious.

"Hi, Dylan. Don't tell me they want me."

"No." He grimaced. "I have something to ask you."

Viveca smiled and sat up. "Well, it can't be as bad as all that. What is it?"

"About Sunday night."

"The Oscar awards?"

"Yeah."

"What about it?"

Dylan shook his head and kicked shit. "I feel really funny asking you this."

Viveca patted the bed beside her. "Sit down, Dylan. You're way too nice a guy to be so troubled. What is it?"

He sat down and took a breath. "I know there's not a chance in hell, and I feel bad about asking, but is there any way you could get me there?"

Viveca's mouth fell open. She blinked. "You want to go to the Oscars?"

"Yeah."

"Oh, my goodness. No wonder you're so nervous about asking. Do you know how hard it is to get a ticket to the Oscars? I'm a nominee, and I wasn't sure they were going to give me a ticket."

Dylan sighed. "Oh, boy. I'm so embarrassed."

"I'm kidding you, Dylan." She chucked him under the chin. "Hey, cheer up. It's not the end of the world. I have a feeling you have a long career ahead of you, and there will be a lot of other Oscars."

"I wanted to see you win."

"That's very sweet. The only way I could take you would be as my date, and I have a date. And, cute as you are, I'm not dumping my boyfriend for you."

"Of course." Dylan stood up. But still he didn't leave. "Look. You know the ropes. Is there any other way I could get in? Anyone else I could ask? Anything else I could do?"

Viveca looked at him and sighed.

"Aw, gee."

Peter Barrington was surprised. Viveca had never acted like a diva before. Throughout the entire production, she had been nothing but professional, cooperative, a joy to work with. For an actress with her credits, her behavior was exemplary and unprecedented. Which was why the request caught him completely off guard.

"You want Dylan at the awards?"

"I know it's a lot to ask."

"And I'm the wrong **person** to ask."

"Well, your movie is up for a zillion awards. Granted, I'm not in it, but I'm in your current movie, and he's been acting as my assistant."

"Won't you be sitting with the cast from **Paris Fling?**"

"I'm the only actor nominated from the movie. I'll be sitting with the director, who's up against you. I hope that's not a problem."

Peter grinned and waved it away. "Trust me on that. So, if you want to take Dylan as your date, it's got nothing to do with me."

"I have a date. My boyfriend is taking me. I have no romantic designs on Dylan. He's just so eager to be there, and has been such a tremendous help to me on the set. It occurred to me, if I happened to win, I could use an assistant backstage to take care of the trophy, shield me from publicity, and get me back in the audience in time for best picture to be announced. I wondered if you could make that happen. He doesn't have to be seated with me. In fact, it would be better if he wasn't. But if he could be anywhere in the theater. Standing room, even, in the back of the audience or in the wings."

She smiled. "I know this puts you in an awkward position. Tessa is nominated for the same award. I'd like to win, but if I can't, I certainly hope it's her. We're all kind of a big family, and Dylan's part of it."

She smiled, self-deprecatingly. "I would hate to be the big-time movie star that he appealed to, who was powerless to do anything. Can you help me out?"

On the morning of the Oscars, Bruce grabbed his car keys and headed out.

Viveca frowned. "Where are you going?"

Bruce shrugged offhandedly. "To the store."

"What for?"

"Beer."

"Beer?"

"To celebrate your Oscar victory."

"You're going to celebrate my Oscar with beer?"

"I like beer."

"I might not win."

"You'll win."

"Aren't you going to get dressed?"

"I am dressed."

"For the ceremony!"

"I'm a guy. It doesn't take me long to get dressed."

"I know, but—"

He was already out the door.

Bruce had commandeered one end of the garage for a workshop, complete with table saw, drill press, and power tools. He unlocked the cabinet and took out the small tool kit, electrical tester, and work permit he'd used before. He locked the cabinet, hopped in the car, and took off.

As he drove, he pulled out his cell phone and called Rachael, the production assistant from the theater who had helped him before. "Hi there, this is the electrical inspector again. I'm on my way to the Palladium for my final check. Do you have the final presentation schedule ready?"

"Yes."

"Great. I'll be there in about fifteen minutes."

Rachael was waiting when he drove up to the theater. He took the time to park legally. The last thing he needed was to get a parking ticket with Viveca's car.

Bruce grabbed his tool kit and hopped out.

Rachael was holding a file folder.

"Is that the schedule?"

She nodded.

Bruce flipped through the file, apparently randomly, being careful to note that the location for the Best Actress award was included. "Perfect. I know my way around now, so I don't need to take up more of your time. I'll check out the connections and be on my way."

Inside, Bruce blended with the people scurrying in all directions making last-minute preparations. He made his way to the front of the auditorium and slipped out the side door near the stage. From there he made his way to the fire door to the stairs below.

Underneath the stage, the catwalks and scaffolding were still in place. Bruce scurried up the ladder to the top. He took the schedule Rachael had given him, and checked it one last time. There was no mistake. The award for Best Actress would be presented from the stage-right microphone.

Bruce worked his way across the catwalk. Sure enough, there on the crossbeam underneath the stage, was the X he'd marked before.

Bruce set his tool kit down on the catwalk, popped it open, and got to work.

When he was finished, Bruce climbed down from the catwalk, went up the stairs, through the fire door, and out a back door.

He was halfway home before he remembered

he'd told Viveca he'd gone out to get beer. He stopped at a convenience store and bought a six-pack.

He drove home, locked his tool kit in the cabinet, grabbed the beer, and went back in the house, hoping that Viveca wouldn't notice how long he'd taken.

He shouldn't have worried. Viveca was busy with hair and makeup preparations, and had barely noticed he was gone.

75

Teddy showed up at Peter Barrington's wearing a tux and carrying a briefcase. Peter met him at the door. "Hey, Mark, come in. You're just in time for a drink."

"Good, I could use one."

Teddy followed Peter into the living room where Ben, Tessa, and Hattie were having drinks. The girls looked stunning in their evening gowns—Tessa in red, and Hattie in gold.

Ben, like Teddy, was wearing a tux. "Hey, what's with the briefcase?" he said. "Isn't that a little out of place?"

"It's not mine," Teddy said. "At least, it's not Mark Weldon's. It's Billy Barnett's. It has a few items from my makeup kit Billy might need. You know Billy, always wants to look his very best."

"You're going to look funny with that on the red carpet," Tessa said.

"Yeah," Hattie said. "They might mistake you for one of the guys from Pricewaterhouse."

"I was hoping one of you could bring it in for me. I don't want to call attention to it. Surely a director or a studio head could have something with him without causing comment?"

"Maybe Dylan could bring it in," Tessa said.

"Dylan?" Teddy said. "Why would Dylan be there?"

"Viveca asked Peter to get Dylan in as her assistant," Tessa said. "I think she has a crush on the boy."

"Don't be catty," Ben said. "You're too nice a person and you're no good at it."

"Dylan won't be with her," Peter said. "She'll be accompanied by her boyfriend."

"Then why is he going?" Teddy said.

"Why, indeed?" Peter said. "Viveca asked for him. I was surprised because she's never made any outrageous demands before."

"I don't think she was trying to be a diva," Tessa said. "She didn't want to be the bad guy who told him he couldn't go."

"Oh?"

"Dylan made a big pitch about really wanting to be there. Which was a ridiculous request, but she didn't like being put in that position."

"So she put me in that position," Peter said. "In any case, he'll be there and could bring your brief-case, if you wanted."

Teddy frowned. "Actually, I don't. The fewer people who know about the briefcase, the better. I particularly don't want anyone to connect it to Mark Weldon or Billy Barnett."

"I can bring it," Ben said. "I'm not nominated for anything. I'm just the lowly studio head."

"Thanks, Ben. Just check it in the coatroom."

"And slip you the claim check?"

"I think you'd better redeem it, too. Otherwise, I'll be redeeming it as one person, and checking it again as another. I think you better redeem it, wait for me to give it back to you, and check it again. If you can bear to miss part of the ceremony. Sorry about this. I never dreamed I'd have to be Billy Barnett and Mark Weldon at the same award ceremony."

"Hell, missing part of the ceremony is a perk." Ben grinned. "Okay, I'll be your bagman."

76

"Limo's here," Bruce called.

Viveca took a breath and checked her makeup mirror one last time. She was nervous, which made her irritated with herself. She was never nervous acting, or even on TV talk shows. She was always calm and relaxed, pleasant and charming. It was just the damn awards. Every time she was nominated she was filled with anxiety. What if she didn't win?

And she hadn't won. She had lost, one Oscar after another, until the prize had seemed further and further from her grasp.

This time was worse. She had won at the Golden Globes, which made the whole thing seem possible.

And then this competition with Tessa was tying her up in knots.

Viveca shook her head to clear it. She pushed back from the makeup table, got up, and went out to the limo.

Bruce was already there, standing by the open back door, waiting to offer assistance with her dress and pack her in. After Viveca was settled, he trotted around the back of the car to hop in the other side. He closed the door and the limo took off.

"You look beautiful," Bruce said.

"Huh?" It took Viveca a moment to register the compliment. She smiled. "Thanks."

Bruce looked good, too, in his tux. She needn't have worried about him. This damn award ceremony had her on edge.

A block from the theater the limo pulled over to let Bruce out, since he wouldn't be accompanying her on the red carpet. At any media event where she might be caught on film, Viveca always presented herself as a femme fatale, available but elusive, the impossible dream.

This was fine with Bruce, who had no desire to deal with the media. He had been avoiding the press even before his PTSD. He opened the door and hopped out.

Viveca leaned across the seat before he could close the door. "You know it's a different theater?"

"I can get in."

"You have your ticket?"

Bruce patted the breast pocket of his tux and smiled. "I have my ticket." He closed the door, and the limo drove off.

Bruce watched it go, then set off down the street.

He had his ticket all right, but that wasn't why he smiled when he patted his pocket.

He also had his cell phone.

77

Teddy and Tessa's limo pulled up to the red carpet on the sidewalk in front of the Grande Palladium Theater, where velvet ropes held back the crowd. Just outside the ropes TV cameras were set up, and spotlights on stanchions made sure the celebrities walking the carpet were well lit.

Teddy—in Mark Weldon guise—hopped out, came around the back of the limo, extended his arm, and ushered Tessa Tweed onto the carpet.

The crowd, who had been moderately excited to see him, went crazy over Tessa. There were cheers and applause, and shouted greetings and well wishes.

Immediately descending on her with a microphone was a woman Teddy recognized as a minor
TV celebrity. Her job was to throw a few introduc-
tory questions, separate the wheat from the chaff,
and guide the A-list movie stars into the presence
of the TV personalities actually hosting the pre-
award show.

As Oscar nominees, Tessa and Mark Weldon
were way at the top of the A-list, and were
immediately thrust into the queue waiting to be
interviewed. There were half a dozen actors and
actresses in the line, some of them quite famous,
but apparently none of them nominees, and an
executive producer type appeared out of nowhere
and escorted Teddy and Tessa to the front of
the line.

The interviewers were a man and a woman
who cohosted some national talk show or another.
Teddy vaguely recalled them being known as Judy
and Jake, the type of cute billing associated with
the early-morning shows.

Judy recognized them first. "Look who's here!
Tessa Tweed and Mark Weldon, the stars of
Desperation at Dawn!"

Teddy and Tessa smiled and nodded. Teddy
hoped that was all that would be required of him.
It appeared that it might be. Judy immediately
pounced on Tessa as the prime interview.

"Tessa Tweed, as a relative newcomer, what does it feel like to be nominated for Best Actress in a Motion Picture?"

Tessa smiled. "Totally unreal. I feel like I'm going to wake up at any moment and find myself in a high school production of **Our Town**, dreaming of what it would be like to be a Hollywood actress."

"Well, you're way beyond that," Judy said. "You've reached the big time. How do you plan to celebrate if you win?"

"Oh, goodness," Tessa demurred. "I don't expect to, so haven't made any plans. It's an honor just to be nominated."

"Here's Mark Weldon," Jake said. "Nominated for Best Supporting Actor for playing one of the scariest bad guys in motion-picture history. I'm nervous just talking to him. Tell me, Mark, does a part like that come easy to you?"

Teddy smiled. "Not at all. I'm just a big pussycat."

"So what do you do to get in character?"

Teddy shrugged. "I'm a method actor. Before we start filming, I like to go out and kill as many people as possible."

Jake looked stunned for a moment, then burst out laughing. "And there you have it. Mark Weldon's secret for success. Very funny, Mark. Do I see a comedy or two in your future?"

"I wouldn't count me out," Teddy said. He smiled and ushered Tessa on into the theater.

The auditorium was nearly three-quarters full. Teddy and Tessa walked down the aisle to the front, where the stars and nominees sat.

Their seats were in the fourth row, just off the aisle. As they sat down, Teddy could see Peter and Hattie and Ben seated in the row behind them.

There was an empty seat next to Peter Barrington. That was Billy Barnett's seat.

The producer was going to be late.

78

In the greenroom underneath the stage, Rachael Quigly watched the Oscar preshow on a monitor, along with other low-ranking members of the crew. She could have watched at home, but it was a thrill just being in the theater, even if she couldn't see the live show, even if she was just watching it on TV.

And she was nervous, had been ever since she had handled the electrical inspector. In the back of her mind was the nagging doubt: What if something goes wrong and it was her fault? Not that she had done anything, but was there anything she didn't do? Should she have double-checked the inspection, got someone else's stamp of approval on the job? Of course not. Her boss was already harried and would have been irritated with her, an assistant who couldn't even hold a clipboard without instructions.

On the TV screen, Viveca Rothschild was being interviewed.

For some reason she didn't seem happy.

Viveca was quick to plaster the smile back on her face, but it was clear she was doing her best not to wince.

The interviewer had just said, "Third time's the charm."

"That's an old saying, Judy," Viveca said, "but it's different every time. There are five nominees, and there's no one who doesn't deserve it. In the end it's up to the people who voted."

Judy beamed. "And there you have it. Viveca Rothschild, gracious as ever."

Jake jumped in. "Viveca, I understand you're currently filming with two other Oscar nominees. What's that like, a little friendly rivalry?"

"Accent on friendly, Jake. I have never been in a production where the actors were so willing to throw their egos overboard and work for the good of the film. Don't be surprised if you see some of us back here next year."

"Nice," Jake said. "A prediction for next year's Academy Awards. Remember, you heard it here first. Thank you, Viveca."

Viveca escaped from the clutches of the interviewers, and pressed on into the theater. Being a nominee, her seat was near the front of the house. Her producer, director, and some of the other actors from **Paris Fling** were already seated in the row. She slipped into her seat, accepting hugs, kisses, and congratulations.

Bruce wasn't there yet.

Viveca wondered if he'd gotten lost.

79

Gino Patelli couldn't believe how far he was from the stage. "I'm a producer and you couldn't get better seats than this?"

"This is Hollywood," Sylvester told him. "Everyone and his brother is a producer. Most of them couldn't get seats at all."

"Where's our boy?"

"He's not here yet."

"You sure?"

"He hasn't made contact."

"I don't like it. He should be here."

"He'll be here."

"Where's Barnett?"

"Up front with the rest of the nominees."

"Do you see him?"

"You can't see him from here."

"Then how do you know where he is?"

Sylvester bit back a sigh. "I don't know that he is here yet, but that's where his seat will be. He's a producer of a nominated picture, so he's going to sit in it."

"Go check."

Sylvester got up and walked down the aisle. He had no trouble spotting the people from Billy Barnett's film. The actors were there, and the director, and some of the others he'd seen in the restaurant.

The producer was not there.

Sylvester turned around and went back to his seat.

"Well?" Gino demanded.

"He's not here yet."

Gino exhaled angrily. "Son of a bitch!"

80

Sherry Day was nervous. That wasn't how Oscar night was supposed to be. In her imaginings, the evening would be filled with wonder and excitement. Instead, it was just a source of apprehension. She had no idea who Sylvester was sending as her date. That was all right, but she at least expected to meet him.

She had been asked to drop his ticket off with the receptionist at a business in East L.A. The company turned out to be a salvage business. The receptionist turned out to be a burly mechanic manning the desk in between tune-ups and tranny repairs. She hoped he wasn't her date.

She'd arrived at the theater alone, gone through security, had her ticket scanned, and been ushered to her seat, which was, as she expected, fairly near the back. Of course, the fact that she was in row W was something of a hint. There was a couple to her left, and a couple one seat over to her right. The seat immediately to her right was vacant.

It was nearly time for the telecast. She wondered if her date was even going to show. Suddenly, there he was, a slender man in a business suit, not a tux, but a perfectly respectable suit and tie. The people in the row stood up to let him through. He squeezed by and dropped into the seat next to Sherry.

She favored him with a smile. "There you are. I was wondering if you were going to make it."

"Why wouldn't I make it?"

"I don't know. I don't know you. I'm Sherry."

He nodded, then realized something was expected of him. "Bob," he said.

He did not offer his hand. Taking the cue, she did not offer hers. "Are you in the industry?"

He blinked. "Industry?"

"The movie business."

"No."

"I am. I'm an actress."

"Yes," he said. He made no attempt to continue the conversation. He ignored her completely and scanned the room, as if looking for someone. After a while he got up, pushed his way out of the row, and walked down the aisle, craning his neck.

Sherry took a deep breath and exhaled slowly.

This was going to be a long evening.

Sylvester's cell phone pulsed. He tugged it out of his pocket and clicked it on. "Yes?"

It was the shooter. "He's not here."

"I know he's not here."

"If he doesn't show, the deal is off."

"Trust me, he'll show. He may be late, but he'll be here."

"And how will I know? I can't be wandering up and down the aisles during the telecast to check if he's here yet."

"I have a plan. Watch me now," Sylvester said.

"I can't see you from my seat. Watch you what?"

"Watch the aisle."

Sylvester slipped out of his seat and walked up the aisle toward the back of the theater. He could see the shooter sitting next to Sherry Day.

He spoke into his cell phone. "See me now?"

"Yes." The shooter hissed it through clenched teeth.

"Keep watching. Pay attention to the young man I talk to."

Sylvester clicked the phone off and kept going to the back of the audience to the standing section. He picked Dylan out of the crowd and pulled him aside.

"When Billy Barnett arrives, during the next commercial break I want you to hurry down the aisle, shake his hand, and say, 'Glad you made it, I just wanted to say congratulations.' Try to get him to stand up when you shake his hand."

"I can't do that," Dylan said.

"Slow learner? You can do anything I tell you to do. When he comes in, you do it. No excuses. No second chances. Get it done."

Sylvester turned around and headed back to his seat. On the way he buzzed the shooter.

"You see the kid I talked to?"

"Yeah."

"Good. Here's what he's going to do."

81

As the show began, the lights dimmed, a huge screen was lowered over the stage, and the picture popped on. It was a shot of the Oscar host, incredibly popular TV personality Jeremy Jenkins. With a background in Broadway theater, feature films, and standup comedy, Jeremy had already hosted the Tonys and the Emmys, and this was his first go at the Academy Awards.

On the screen, Jeremy is lying in bed. His eyes pop open. His face registers terror. He is late for the awards.

He rushes out the door, ripping off his pajamas, and bursts into the street, wearing a strange-looking tuxedo with no opening in the front. He stops, looks over his shoulder. He has put it on backward. He grabs his head, gives it a 180-degree twist. He looks down to see his bow tie is now under his chin. He nods in satisfaction and sprints for his car.

He speeds down the freeway, hits a traffic jam, hops out of his car, and runs along the roofs of the other cars toward the theater.

He arrives at the theater where a group of anxious singers and dancers are waiting to usher him in. They all surge through the theater doors as—

The lights came up on stage, the screen was hauled up, and the scene the audience had been watching seamlessly blended into a live-action opening number performed by Jeremy and the chorus.

The song and dance was pleasant, if unsensational. At best, it let Jeremy get off a few one-liners. At worst, it resembled a slightly under-rehearsed Broadway routine.

In the ensuing applause, Jeremy launched into his opening monologue. As was his custom, he singled out some of the nominees to pick on. Teddy prayed he wouldn't be one of them, but of course he was.

Jeremy's face lit up in recognition. "I see Mark Weldon is here tonight," he said happily. His face froze and he put up his hand and edged away. "And I'm not going to say a thing about him," he said, and the audience laughed appreciatively.

Jeremy finished his opening monologue and segued straight into the awards. As usual, Best Supporting Actor was first, a high-profile award to grab the audience's attention before the lull to follow.

"Ladies and gentlemen," Jeremy announced. "To present the Best Supporting Actor award, here is last year's Best Supporting Actress, Susan Rifkin."

The attractive young actress came out displaying a daringly stylish V-necked ball gown, cut to the navel. She stepped up to the stage-right microphone stand and read from the teleprompter.

"And the nominees are: Mark Weldon, for **Desperation at Dawn.**"

On the TV screen, the shot of Susan Rifkin at the microphone cut to a shot of Teddy Fay sitting in the audience. It immediately shrunk to a headshot that appeared in a little square box in one corner of the picture of Susan. As she read off the names of the other nominees, four more square headshots framed her on the screen.

Susan smiled and ripped the envelope open.

"And the winner is . . . Mark Weldon, **Deperation at Dawn!**"

Teddy was stunned. The next thing he knew his friends were pounding him on the back, and Tessa was laughing and pushing him out of his seat.

"Get up! Get up! You won!"

Teddy walked toward the stage as if in a daze. He went up the steps on automatic pilot, accepted the award, and suddenly found himself at the microphone. He hadn't prepared any remarks, not expecting to win.

So he started with that.

"This is a surprise. There were four other deserving nominees, and I was happy just to be named with them." He looked around, realized something more was expected. "All I can say is this must be very encouraging to all the stuntmen working out there. And I'm happy to pass along the secret to my success. Get yourself cast in a Peter Barrington film, and play all your scenes with Tessa Tweed. Thank you."

Teddy started back toward his seat, but was immediately intercepted by an attractive but efficient young woman in an evening gown who linked her arm in his and guided him offstage into the wings.

Backstage photographers and TV crews were waiting to pounce. Teddy was whisked through a door into a room soundproofed from the stage where they could have a go at him.

It was never-ending. No sooner did one group finish with him than another group would pounce. He couldn't be rude to them and excuse himself. If he didn't cooperate, suddenly the big story would be what an ungracious winner he was.

The only saving grace was that there were monitors everywhere, so he could tell just where they were in the show. For all the time the interviews were taking, it didn't seem like they had gotten very far. After the Best Supporting Actor and Supporting Actress awards, there was a long gap in the ceremony before they got back to anything major.

The show was just coming up on the first-hour break when Teddy was finally ushered back to his seat.

Peter leaned over and tapped him on the shoulder. "Did you make another movie out there?"

"No, I just explained why people liked this one."

"What did you tell them?"

"There's no accounting for taste."

Peter nodded. "Glowing. We should use that in the ads."

Ben lowered his voice and asked, "When do you want to go?"

Teddy looked at his watch. "In about half an hour I'll go out. Wait a few minutes, so it doesn't look like we're going together, then you go."

"Oh," Ben said. "So, now that you're an Oscar winner, you can boss the head of the studio around?"

"Relax," Teddy said. "We can talk about my new trailer later."

On the next half-hour commercial break Teddy got up and headed for the men's room. He went in, accepted congratulations from some actor he didn't know, and spent a couple of minutes washing his hands to let the actor leave first.

Teddy came out and headed in the direction of the coat check in the lobby. Ben met him halfway and handed him the briefcase.

Teddy held up his hand, fingers spread. "Five minutes."

"I'll be here."

The men's room was empty, but Teddy didn't dare use one of the mirrors over the sinks in case someone should walk in. He took the briefcase into a toilet stall, sat down, popped the case open on his lap, and took out a makeup mirror.

The transformation from Mark Weldon to Billy Barnett wasn't that hard. The hair sold it. Mark Weldon's hair was dark brown, nearly black, as fit his image. Billy Barnett's hair was naturally gray. Mark Weldon's hair was a wig, but the high-quality workmanship was unmatched. Few people had any idea it wasn't real hair.

Teddy put the finishing touches on the makeup, snapped the briefcase shut, and came out of the stall. He double-checked his appearance in the mirror over the sink. All was in order.

Teddy came out of the men's room to find Ben waiting for him. He handed him the briefcase.

"Billy Barnett," Ben said. "Just the man I wanted to see."

"Oh?"

"You have to have a talk with one of your actors." Ben shook his head. "Guy won an Oscar, now he wants a trailer upgrade."

83

Dylan's mouth fell open.

Billy Barnett was coming down the aisle, large as life. He was already halfway back to his seat. Why couldn't Dylan have spotted him earlier, intercepted him on his way down the aisle? That would have been so much more natural than accosting him in his seat. It just wasn't done. Not by a lowly gofer.

But there was no help for it. It was a case of do it or else. Dylan swallowed hard, and started down the aisle.

Dylan walked straight up to the row where Billy Barnett sat. He leaned in and said, "Mr. Barnett?"

Teddy stood up and leaned over. "Yes?"

"I didn't see you before, and I just wanted to say congratulations on your Oscar nomination."

Dylan extended his hand.

Teddy shook it.

Dylan headed back up the aisle.

Teddy sat back down and frowned.

What the hell?

Teddy Fay was on high alert. Dylan had just marked him as a target, Teddy was sure of it. He had spent too much time in the CIA not to recognize the action for what it was. The kid had made him uneasy all along, and now his suspicions were confirmed.

Teddy scanned the room for danger, for anybody taking a particular interest in him or his costars. Mike Freeman's men had gotten Tessa Tweed to the Academy Awards. It was his job to protect her while she was there.

As well as protect himself.

During the next commercial break Teddy said, "Excuse me," got up, and walked the aisle. He saw Gino Patelli and his henchman. They pretended not to see him, or at least not to care. Their elaborate indifference was almost comical.

Teddy continued on up the aisle.

A man near the back of the orchestra section looked like a pro. He wasn't doing anything wrong, but Teddy had a sixth sense about people, and this guy's posture and expression marked him as someone familiar with casual violence. Judging from the way his jacket hung, Teddy could tell the man wasn't wearing a gun, so whatever threat he might pose was not immediate.

Teddy reached the end of the aisle. Dylan was there in the standing-room-only crowd. His eyes widened as he saw Teddy heading in his direction.

Teddy stopped as if he had just remembered something, went back down the aisle, and sat with Tessa Tweed.

Okay. He'd identified the players.

What was the game?

84

Desperation at Dawn picked up a second Oscar when Hattie won Best Original Score for her hauntingly beautiful jazzy music that echoed the great noir films of the forties and fifties. Not being an actress, she was allowed to return to her seat.

She had barely sat down when Peter picked up an Oscar for Best Original Screenplay, making them a two-Oscar family. No one wanted to interview a screenwriter, either, and he sat down to the congratulations of his friends.

Aside from that, the ceremony was uneventful. A Lifetime Achievement Award was presented to an actor so old his entire acceptance speech was inaudible and unintelligible.

Amazingly, he was the highlight. The rest of the show was pretty boring, with the exception of the Best Foreign Film. The director, a flamboyant Frenchman, picked up the microphone stand as if he were a rock star and danced around the stage with it, burbling effusively in French. No one attempted to translate, and no one had the faintest idea what he was saying.

Finally he finished talking, put the microphone down, and paraded off-stage, waving the Oscar aloft.

Jeremy thankfully regained control of the show, and took it to commercial.

Bruce was practically jumping out of his seat. That idiot! That damn Frenchman had moved the microphone! Why, of all things, did he have to pick up the microphone?

And not put it back in the right place!

It was off-center, maybe three or four feet. Bruce told himself it didn't matter. Surely the stagehands would put it back.

Only they didn't. They gave out the next award from the same spot.

They went to a commercial and no stagehands came out. No one went near the microphone. It was late, the awards were wearing on, the musical numbers were all done, and there was nothing left to set up. There couldn't be many awards left—it was almost over, and when they came back from commercial, they would give out Best Actress, and everything would be ruined.

Bruce stood up and pushed his way to the aisle. With a few quick steps he reached the stage, picked up the microphone stand, and put it back on its spot. He adjusted the microphone, turned, and went back down the steps just as if he had every right to be there and was doing exactly what he was supposed to be doing. He squeezed his way back into the row and sat down.

Viveca was astounded. Bruce's behavior was sometimes erratic, but it always made sense in one way or another. This was just bizarre.

"Bruce!" she whispered. "What are you doing?"

"Helping."

"Why did you move the microphone?"

"It was in the wrong place."

"What?"

"That French guy moved it."

"What does it matter?"

"You're not going to make your acceptance speech from the wrong place."

"But—"

"Don't worry. It's all right."

85

Teddy was confused. Viveca's young man had gone up on stage and moved the microphone, a totally bizarre gesture that had to mean something. Teddy had already connected Bruce to the death of the gossip columnist, and while he'd never seen Bruce and Dylan the gofer together, they were connected through Viveca.

He was up to something.

There was danger, but it was spread out among Gino Patelli and his henchman, the potential hit man in the audience, and Viveca's young man sitting just two rows away.

If anything was going to happen, it would happen soon. The Oscars were winding down. Peter had picked up his second Oscar for Best Director, which meant the Best Actor and Actress categories were coming up. After that it was Best Picture. That was the moment of most danger. It would happen then, as all the producers and writers and director and actors would mob the stage to celebrate the acceptance of the award. It would happen in that confusion.

If **Desperation at Dawn** won, they would all be on stage, easy targets. If another picture won, the mob on stage would attract attention away from those left in the audience. Teddy and his friends would be sitting ducks. That was the only possible instance in which the man he had marked as a potential danger might strike.

He considered walking the aisle to make sure the man he'd spotted earlier was still in his seat.

Before he could move, the music swelled and they were back from commercial.

86

Jeremy Jenkins looked smug. The telecast had gone great. All his rehearsed bits were over. The songs and dances, always problematic when done live, had gone smoothly. His monologue had scored, his ad-libs had gone over well, and he had nothing left to do but introduce the presenters of the final awards. He did so with a flourish, as if he were personally responsible for the star status of the celebrities he was introducing.

"And now, ladies and gentlemen, to present the award for Best Actress, here is last year's Best Actor winner, Richard Kessington."

The handsome young actor, sporting the

practically obligatory beard, walked onto the stage and stepped up to the microphone. He didn't bother with a joke. There was no reason to run the risk of bombing, and due to his star status he didn't need to.

"The nominees for Best Actress in a Motion Picture are: Viveca Rothschild, for **Paris Fling** . . ."

On a monitor behind him the square inset of Viveca sitting in the audience appeared. She was smiling and nodding, but she seemed clearly distracted and her eyes were stealing glances to her left.

A s soon as Richard began to read the names, Bruce rose from his seat and edged his way out of the row toward the side aisle. His exit had been seen momentarily in Viveca's headshot when the camera cut to her, as had the surprise on her face when he got up.

Bruce reached the far aisle. He plastered himself to the wall, worked his way toward the stage, and went out the side exit just as Richard read the name of the last nominee.

"And Tessa Tweed, for **Desperation at Dawn**."

. . . .

Bruce's heart was pounding. He had to hurry. The damn actor presenting the award wasn't wasting any time with it. He'd rattled through the names of the nominees as if he had a plane to catch. He was probably already ripping open the envelope. Any second he'd say, "And the winner is . . ."

Bruce pushed the fire door open and went down the stairs to the area under the stage. He couldn't see a monitor, but the audio was on speakers everywhere so there wasn't a chance that he would miss it. Any moment now the actor would say the winner's name.

He prayed it would be Viveca.

Rachael Quigly had a lump in her throat. What the hell was going on? She was still in the greenroom watching the Oscars with the performers and production people, and it had been a lot of fun. The show was nearly over, at which point she would be able to sneak upstairs in her ball gown and mingle with the movie stars as the theater emptied out.

Suddenly it was as if she'd been kicked in the head by a mule. The presenter, Richard Kessington, had read the name of the nominee, Viveca Rothschild, and as the camera cut to her, the young man sitting next to her got up from his seat. It was just a second and he was gone. The camera, of course, stayed on Viveca.

Even so.

She recognized him. She was sure of it. The man sitting next to Viveca Rothschild was the electrical inspector she had shown around the theater.

She told herself it couldn't be. Some people looked like each other, and she was dealing with the movie business where people were **made** to look like each other. She expected role-playing, make-believe, pretend.

She'd no sooner convinced herself she was mistaken than she saw him again, coming down the stairs.

87

And the winner is, Tessa Tweed!"

The applause was deafening. Tessa Tweed clearly was a popular choice. She rose from her seat, a look of wonder on her face, as her friends patted her on the back and cheered her on.

Teddy was pleased, but cautiously so. He couldn't help glancing over at Viveca to see how she was taking it. It was hard to tell. Her face was averted, and she was looking in the direction where her boyfriend had gone.

As Tessa started up the aisle, Teddy scanned the audience for trouble. His eyes kept coming back to Viveca. She looked around now at Tessa Tweed, and her look was not one of jealousy or envy or anger, it was of alarm and concern.

She rose from her seat. "Tessa!" she cried, but the words were swept away in the thunderous applause.

Bruce pulled his cell phone out of his pocket. This was it. The worst had happened. Viveca had lost yet again, and her damn costar would be walking up on stage at any moment.

He'd promised Viveca she would not see Tessa Tweed accept the award, and he would keep his word. He reached the bottom of the stairs.

A gaggle of men and women were clustered around a monitor. He watched as Tessa Tweed received hugs and congratulations from the people around her, and began to walk toward the stage.

Suddenly a young woman in an evening dress disengaged herself from the group. Her eyes were wide, a look of incredulity on her face. She seemed familiar, though in that moment he could hardly have cared. His attention was drawn to the monitor, and—

He suddenly realized. It was that damn production assistant who'd shown him around the theater.

It had never occurred to him that she'd be here, but here she was, and apparently she recognized him.

He turned and walked away, hoping she wouldn't follow. He could no longer see the monitor, but it didn't matter, he could hear the audio. His cell phone still had a clear line to the detonator. Practically anywhere beneath the stage would do.

88

Teddy sprang from his seat. The moment he saw Viveca call out to Tessa, he had the picture. Viveca's boyfriend—a troubled man with combat experience—was championing her, protecting her, defending her from all harm. He saw Tessa as a potential rival, and was doing his best to destroy her. He'd killed the gossip columnist to cover up his involvement in the attempt to tear Tessa down and make Viveca win. All else having failed, he'd planned one last desperate move. It involved making sure the microphone at stage right was in a specific location.

Teddy sprinted down the aisle and skipped up the steps ahead of Tessa, as if he were some insane rock star about to claim Tessa's Grammy for his own. He threw his arm about Richard Kessington, whispered, "Change of venue," and, jabbing his thumb into a pressure point, marched the young man from the stage-right microphone stand to the microphone stand at stage left.

Tessa, baffled by his behavior, nonetheless altered her course and met them at the microphone. Teddy stepped back and cautiously allowed Richard Kessington to present her with the award. She took it, stepped to the microphone, and said, understandably, "Oh, my God!"

Bruce heard Tessa's voice on the monitor. He aimed his cell phone and pressed the button.

An explosion rocked the theater. The stage-right microphone stand became shrapnel, hurtling in all directions.

Teddy threw himself in front of Tessa, shielding her body with his own. He could feel jagged bits of metal penetrating his skin. He crashed to the stage floor, pulling Tessa down with him, his arms shielding her face. He sensed the presenter, blown off his feet, falling upstage behind them. Teddy rolled on top of Tessa, protecting her from harm.

In the greenroom people were screaming and running, terrified by the debris falling from the hole in the stage above. Only Rachael stood her ground, transfixed and horrified at the sight of the young man she had known as an inspector, who had just activated a bomb. As she gawked at him, his eyes locked on hers.

Rachael turned and ran. She mixed herself in with the actors in the greenroom, praying that there was safety in numbers, that he would not be able to thin her out of the herd. She didn't look to see if he was following, she just ran as fast as she could, up the stairs and out the door to daylight.

89

A quick once-over told Teddy that while Tessa was rightly terrified, she was not hurt. He helped her to her feet and led her away from the cavernous burned-out hole in the stage.

People were screaming and fleeing the theater. Naturally, it was those closest to the stage who reacted first, so a wave of movie stars were jamming the aisles and trying to get out.

Gino Patelli and Sylvester pushed their way through the crowd.

"Did you do that?" Gino said.

"Hell, no."

"Did he?"

"He's a shooter, not a bomber."

"Where is he?"

The shooter was gone. At the first sign of trouble he had slipped out of the building. It didn't matter that he hadn't the slightest thing to do with it, the shooter was a professional. He wasn't about to be questioned by the police under any circumstances. As in any emergency, he was the first one out the door.

The shooter had his equipment in the trunk of his car out front, in case he was able to make the ID and line up a shot as people were leaving. That wasn't an option with half the police in L.A. descending on the theater. Sirens and flashing lights were coming from all directions as he drove off into the night.

Of all the people in the theater, only Peter, Ben, and Hattie were rushing **toward** that tragedy. They surged up onto the stage, intercepting Teddy and Tessa.

Ben's face was a picture of anguish. "My God, are you all right?"

Tessa showed her Best Actress Oscar was no fluke. For Ben's sake, she mustered a smile. "Never better," she said, then fell into his arms.

The police weren't easy to deal with. They insisted on dragging all the principals down to the station for witness statements. By principals, they seemed to mean "famous movie people," Viveca and Tessa and Billy Barnett chief among them. They'd have dragged Mark Weldon in, too, but they couldn't find him. They found that highly suspicious.

The police let Tessa go almost immediately. She was clearly the intended victim, not the perpetrator, and she had cuts and bruises that needed to be attended to. After a few questions, she was released to the paramedics standing by with an ambulance.

Teddy had cuts and bruises, too, but no one seemed to care.

Teddy gave his statement several times. The police kept coming back to what had motivated him to go up on stage and move Tessa's Oscar acceptance speech from one microphone to the other. His answer did not thrill them, the fact that it was the simple truth notwithstanding. Viveca Rothschild's young man had moved the microphone stand, and then left the theater just before the award. The cops couldn't believe that was enough evidence from which to deduce foul play. The fact that no cop on the force would have made that deduction did not help. And Teddy, as movie producer Billy Barnett, could not point to a lifetime of experience in the CIA to explain why his judgment was better.

One thing in his favor was that Bruce was gone; the cops couldn't find him, and Viveca had no idea where he was. She admitted that he had become obsessive lately about her winning the Oscar, and promised her no one else would win. When he left the theater, she had panicked, not knowing what he might do.

"That's why I shouted a warning to Tessa. I thought he might do something."

"Like set a bomb?"

"Good heavens, no. Like drop a sandbag on her head. Because he moved the mic. I come from a theater background, so that was my first thought. Line her up and drop a sandbag on her head."

"You thought that then?"

"Not when he moved the mic. Later, when he got up and left the theater. I thought he was going backstage to untie a rope and drop a sandbag."

That statement sent the cops back to Teddy.

"Did you suspect the boyfriend was going to drop a sandbag or set off a bomb?"

"I didn't suspect either one. I took precautions against **any** foul play."

"Why?"

Teddy had had enough. "Because I find it more productive than taking precautions against **fair** play."

The officer scowled.

There was a knock on the door, and a young detective stuck his head in. He had a rather frightened-looking young woman in tow.

"Yes?" the officer barked.

"Sorry, sir. There's a young woman here I think you should see."

91

Rachael Quigly was exhausted. It was nearly two in the morning when she finished making her statement. The police didn't believe her story, or at least that was the impression she got in the beginning. By the time she was done, her story was harder to dispute. At least their attitude had changed. In the beginning they treated her like she was lying. By the end they treated her like she was an idiot.

She felt like an idiot. She had let herself be duped, and nearly caused a woman's death. All she wanted to do was get home, tear off her clothes, and cry herself to sleep. She paid off the cab, unlocked the downstairs door of her modest second-story walk-up apartment, and dragged herself up the stairs, wishing for once that she had an elevator. Her convertible couch hadn't been pulled out into a bed. She didn't bother doing that now. She hung her ball gown in the closet, flung herself down on the couch, and pulled her comforter up to her neck.

She was too keyed up to sleep. She couldn't stop her mind. She wondered how long it would be before she got up and pulled out the couch.

Bruce crouched in the shadows. He was calm. This was a guerrilla operation, and he was used to those. The young PA could connect him to the bomb. She stood between him and his chance to return home and resume his life with Viveca. With her out of the way, he'd be safe. His disordered mind hadn't registered that he'd amassed so much suspicion from so many people that there was no way his life could remain the same.

Bruce slipped out of the alley where he'd parked his car, crossed the street, and examined the front door. It was flimsy, at best. A thief would have no problem picking it. Bruce was no thief. He pushed hard with both hands and the door popped open.

Rachael's apartment was on the second floor. He'd seen the light go on when she got home. It was a piece of cake. Her apartment door would be locked, but there was a fire escape at the end of the hall, and it ran right by her window.

Bruce started up the stairs.

The next thing he knew he was on his face on the floor. Something cold and hard poked him behind his ear. He didn't have to be told it was a gun.

"Sorry, Bruce," Teddy said. "It's not your night."

Teddy walked Bruce back to the alley from which he'd emerged. He took away his car keys and locked him in the trunk. He drove the car up into the hills overlooking the ocean, pulled off the road, and got out.

Knowing Bruce was an ex-marine, Teddy was careful unlocking the trunk. He was prepared for Bruce to come out swinging, but the young man was subdued, compliant. If anything, he seemed baffled.

He blinked at Teddy and said almost plaintively, "I don't understand."

"What?"

"You're a producer."

Teddy was dressed as Billy Barnett. "So?"

"How could you do this?"

"What did you think producers did?" Teddy shook his head. "You're unlucky, Bruce. You picked the wrong producer. You killed Manny Rosen, didn't you?"

"Who?"

"The gossip columnist. So he wouldn't tell anyone about the stories you planted smearing Tessa Tweed."

"I didn't plant any stories."

So that had been Viveca. "I know you were protecting Viveca, making sure that if she didn't win the award, no one else would have it. See, I know all that. So killing this witness wasn't going to do you any good. Or Viveca, either."

Bruce looked forlorn and confused, as if there was no accounting for how he'd wound up in this place, under these circumstances. Teddy almost felt sorry for the man.

With one swift motion Teddy brought the butt of the gun down on Bruce's head.

Teddy backed the car up and aimed it at the cliff. He wrestled Bruce into position behind the wheel. He revved the engine, slipped the car into gear, stepped back, and slammed the door.

The car plowed straight through the guardrail

and hurtled over and down. It hit the bottom and burst into flames.

Teddy watched for a moment to make sure no flaming figure miraculously staggered out of the wreck. None did. He turned and walked down the mountain.

About two miles away Teddy figured it was far enough. He stopped at a driveway, took out a burner phone he carried for just such purposes, and called an Uber.

93

The cops were a little more interested in Teddy's theories this time.

"I don't know what I can tell you about Bruce's death. I don't know any more than you do."

"Are you surprised he did it?"

"You can't say for sure that he committed suicide. He could just as easily have lost control and driven his car off the road."

"You think it was just a coincidence?"

"I wouldn't say coincidence. The young man had a lot on his mind. It was bound to affect his driving." Teddy cocked his head. "Are we about done?"

"I'll tell you when we're done."

"You keep going over the same ground. You

pulled me off the set. No big deal, I'm a producer, they can film without me. But you have Viveca Rothschild down the hall, and she's got scenes this morning."

"That's too bad. This happens to be an attempted murder."

"She didn't do it."

"Oh, no? C-four was found in her house."

"Where was it?"

The detective didn't answer.

"You didn't find it in any part of the house connected to her, did you? You found it in Bruce's exercise room, or a workshop, someplace only he would have used. That's why you're so desperately questioning Vivcca, to find some way you can connect it to her. Which you couldn't do, even if she didn't have a team of lawyers throwing roadblocks in your path and making your life a holy hell."

The detective scowled.

Teddy grinned. "If I were you, I'd let me go, so you can sneak down the hall and get a look at her. I know it's been distracting you the whole interview to think your buddies got a blonde Hollywood starlet and you're stuck with me."

"Don't be silly," the detective said, but he seemed to be considering it.

Teddy pressed his advantage. "If you do kick me loose, the least you guys could do is drive me back to the set. You pulled me off it, so I don't have a car."

There was a knock on the door, and an officer stuck his head in. "They're going to let the girl go. They said you'd want to know."

The detective frowned.

Teddy suppressed a grin.

In the hallway Officer Murphy took out his cell phone and called Sylvester. "Billy Barnett."

"What about him?"

"The cops brought him in for questioning. He's here now."

Sylvester hung up and called the shooter. "Billy Barnett's at the police station."

"You guys are unbelievable."

"What do you mean?"

"Could you be any more outrageous? The Oscars? The police station? Do you think I have a death wish?"

"Just passing along the information."

"Do me a favor. Stop. I don't need your help. Your constant nagging is a pain in the ass. I'll do the job when I do the job, on my schedule, not yours. You got that?"

"Got it."

"And when I do, don't be alarmed if a day goes by and you don't hear from me. I find it advisable to put some distance between the job and the payment, in case someone is trying to run a trace."

"Of course."

"Meanwhile, knock it off with the ridiculous suggestions. The police station, for Christ's sake!"

The shooter snorted and hung up.

The shooter lay flat on the roof on a six-story office building and trained his sniper's rifle on the entrance of the police station, three hundred and fifty yards away.

Who were these amateurs? Did they really think he couldn't find his target?

As the shooter lay thinking that, his target came out the door. His finger tensed on the trigger, then relaxed.

The target was not alone. Billy Barnett was flanked by two uniformed cops and was semi-concealed, flitting in and out of his sights in no predictable manner. It was almost as if the target was aware of the danger and had taken precautionary measures.

Before the assassin could take the shot, the target climbed into the back of a police car, and the cops got in and took off.

The shooter exhaled in exasperation.

All right. At least he knew where they were going.

The shooter rolled over, sat up, and began packing away his rifle.

94

The cops let Teddy off at the set.

Peter was glad to see him. With both Teddy and Viveca gone, he had been reduced to shooting close-ups of Tessa to cut into sequences he'd already shot.

"Thank God you're here," Peter said. He lowered his voice. "Go change into Mark Weldon and you can shoot some scenes with Tessa."

Teddy cocked his head and put up his hand. "I know you're chomping at the bit to get some filming done, and that sounds like a good idea, but actually there's something we ought to do first."

"Oh?"

"We have a bit of a delicate situation here. The police are about to let Viveca go. She'll be back any minute, and you'll be able to shoot anything you want. Before that happens, we need to take care of business.

"If you and Ben and Tessa could meet me in your trailer, I'll walk you through what we need to do."

Viveca was devastated. Bruce was dead, and under the most horrible circumstances. Her lawyers wouldn't let her answer any questions, but from what the police were asking her, it was clear that their theory was that Bruce had killed himself in a fit of remorse, after failing to murder Tessa.

Viveca was racked with guilt. She had set the whole thing in motion. Everything that Bruce did was because of her insecurity, her jealousy, her desperate need to win. She would never have hurt Tessa, even before she came on the picture, even before they became friends. She had wanted her to fail, yes, but she had never wished her any physical harm. It was repulsive. She could not imagine it.

Just as she could not imagine harming Manny Rosen.

Had Bruce done that, too? She hadn't let herself entertain the thought, and yet if Bruce was behind the attack on Tessa, who knew **what** he might have done.

Viveca got back to the set to find the crew just standing around.

"Where is everybody?" she asked the assistant cameraman.

"Taking a break. We couldn't shoot much without you, and Mark is AWOL, too. I think Peter and Tessa are in their trailers."

Viveca went right by her own trailer and knocked on the door of Tessa's. She was too keyed up to wait for an answer, and pushed the door open.

Billy Barnett was sitting there.

Viveca was startled. In her anxious condition, practically anything would have startled her.

"Oh," she said. "Mr. Barnett. I didn't realize you were here. I want to talk to Tessa."

"No, you don't," Billy Barnett said.

"I beg your pardon?"

"You don't have to tell her anything because there's nothing to tell. Your boyfriend, a combat vet with PTSD, had a psychotic break and became convinced your costar was your nemesis. He did his best to tear her down and finally did something drastic, which I'm sure he regretted. He died as a result of the mess he'd gotten himself into. I wouldn't rule out that he deliberately chose to miss that turn."

"Bruce wouldn't do that."

"You have no idea what he might choose to do. You wouldn't have thought he'd bomb a theater, would you? And now you're here to tell Tessa it was all your fault, that it was your jealousy that set all this in motion. Well, Tessa knows you mean her no harm. I know you mean her no harm. And, more important, the police know you mean her no harm. Let's not make anybody believe otherwise. We're putting out a press release, a statement of solidarity stating that filming is going ahead in spite of this horrible tragedy. Let this be a wake-up call to everybody, a reminder that our wounded servicemen coming home from war are not receiving adequate care.

"I've just come from a meeting with Tessa, Ben, and Peter, and they're all agreed. As of right now, this film is dedicated to the memory of Bruce. It will be a single, full-frame screen credit, up front in the main titles. It will come right after the director's credit, in a font as large as his."

Teddy put up his hands. "Now, that's how we're reacting to the incident. Tessa is ready to embrace you with comfort and support. Accept it, then if you're up to it, Peter is chomping at the bit, and there are some scenes of you and Tessa he'd love to shoot. Think you can handle that?"

Viveca straightened and raised her chin. Her eyes were gleaming.

"Point me in the right direction."

96

Teddy had one more thing to do.

Dylan was hanging out by the coffee cart. Teddy walked up behind him and put a hand on his shoulder. Dylan turned around. His face went white.

"You weren't expecting to see me?"

"You're not often here."

Teddy smiled. "And you know that, don't you?"

"What?"

"You shook my hand at the Oscars."

"I wanted to congratulate you. I hadn't seen you, and—"

Teddy put up his hand. "Yeah, yeah. That was the most reluctant congratulations anyone has ever gotten. You looked like you were telling me your puppy died."

Dylan said nothing.

"What have they got on you? Someone must be making you do this. You're clearly not doing it of your own volition."

"I can't."

"It's all right, kid. You don't have to tell me who they are. I can figure that part out. How are they squeezing you?"

"I owe them five hundred dollars."

"You're kidding."

"No."

"Five hundred dollars?"

"They won't let me pay them back."

"They got you the job?"

Dylan nodded. "If I don't do what they say—"

"Yes, I imagine they have all kinds of grisly things planned for you. What did they make you do? Besides shaking my hand?"

"I had to be at the Oscars."

"Obviously. What else?"

"I had to get assigned to the set."

"That couldn't have been easy, you being new and low on the totem pole."

"One of the other assistants got hurt."

"They arranged for that?"

Dylan couldn't meet his eyes. "No."

"Oh. You arranged for that?"

"I feel so bad. I like everyone here. It's like a family."

"Yeah, well, some families are closer than others. You're out of this one."

"Oh."

"You're lucky, Dylan. You're walking out of here because you're just a dumb kid and you thought you had no choice. You got a production car?"

"Yes, I do."

"Not anymore. Give me the keys."

Dylan handed them over.

"Take off and never come back. Leave L.A., you're out of the movie business. If you should come back, I guarantee you, if they don't find you, I will."

Teddy could see Dylan's mind racing. "And don't contact anyone from this movie. If Viveca should come up to me and say, 'What have you done to Dylan?' that will be my cue to do something to Dylan. Do you understand?"

Dylan gulped. "Yes, sir."

"Good. Get the fuck out of here."

97

The shooter watched from a second-story window across the street.

Securing the apartment hadn't been hard. The tenant had come right to the door. The elderly woman was in the midst of explaining that she hadn't ordered anything from Fresh Direct when the shooter slipped a hypodermic needle into her neck. The sedative was harmless and painless. The woman would probably wake up with no recollection of how she had fallen asleep in her favorite overstuffed chair.

The woman had been watching the filming when the doorbell rang, so the window with the most advantageous view was already open. The shooter was using it now.

Billy Barnett climbed into a production car and drove off the set.

The shooter sprang from the window. He threw his sniper's rifle into the soft pool-cue case he carried for that purpose, and went out the door.

His car was parked at a meter right downstairs facing away from the set. He'd left it there for just such an emergency. The shooter flung his rifle and case onto the back seat, hopped in, and pulled out.

Billy Barnett had about a two-block head start. He was driving along casually as if he had no idea anything was wrong, which indeed he shouldn't. The shooter's targets never knew they were being watched. His surveillance was discreet and from a distance.

The shooter closed the gap slightly so as not to get scraped off by any light.

Billy Barnett drove for several blocks and pulled into the parking lot of a diner. He got out of his car and went through the door.

The shooter pulled up next to a fireplug across the street and surveilled the situation. It was actually not bad. His car had tinted windows, so no one would see him lining up a shot through a one-inch crack at the top. For an impromptu duck blind, the car would do quite nicely.

The shooter rolled the window down a crack and retrieved his rifle from the back seat. He double-checked the sight. He had to be ready the second the target came out the door.

The shooter sensed rather than heard the back door of the car opening. He felt the cold steel on the back of his neck.

The shooter's jaw tightened and he smiled. "Well done."

"Glad you approve," Teddy Fay said. "You don't seem afraid."

"I'm not."

"Why?"

"Because I'm a professional and you're an amateur. You think you have the upper hand, but you don't."

"Oh?"

"You're a producer. You like to think you can do anything you want, get away with a murder the same way you'd dodge a parking ticket. But now that you're faced with it, you don't have it in you. If you were going to shoot me, you'd have done it already."

"I don't like to kill in cold blood—it seems unsporting. On the other hand, if you still intend to kill me . . ."

The man's gaze was steady. "I don't think you can stop me."

"You're well trained," Teddy said. "Ex-military or FBI, I would think. Probably not CIA, or I'd know who you are."

The shooter paused. "How? You're a producer."

"I wasn't always. I've done a lot of odd jobs in my day. Anyway, don't beat yourself up over this. I'm sure you're very good. You just ran into bad luck. You can make the safest bet in the world, and once in a blue moon, it doesn't pay off."

The shooter gawked. "Who **are** you?"

"I'm an Oscar-winning producer. Practically invincible."

Teddy shrugged. "So. Make your move."

98

The Oscar for Best Picture was given out live on the early-evening news in L.A., and it went to **Desperation at Dawn**. Peter Barrington accepted the award on behalf of the producers. He thanked the usual people, adding a special thanks to Billy Barnett.

"Billy couldn't be here to accept this award, but no one deserved it more than he. I know he would be proud."

Gino Patelli put the TV on mute. "He got him!"
Sylvester didn't look so sure.

"Barnett won an Oscar but wasn't there to pick it up? I'd say he's out of commission and his team's hiding it to avoid bad press."

"If you say so."

A goon stuck his head in the door. "The car's here." In his capacity as a producer, Gino had received an invitation to a Hollywood party, and was taking the chance to hobnob with the rich and famous.

"I bet everybody will be talking about that damn movie that just won the Oscar," Gino complained.

He and Sylvester made their way out to the car.

Gino couldn't help crabbing about everything. "Did you get a limo?"

"I got a limo."

"Is it a stretch limo?"

"You didn't want a stretch limo."

"So you didn't get a stretch limo?"

"I got the car you always get. You want me to send it away and get you a stretch limo?"

"Let's see what you got."

It was a regular limo. Gino and Sylvester climbed into the back seat and it took off.

"How far is this damn party?" Gino said as they drove out the gate.

"I don't know. They gave the directions to the driver."

"Oh, yeah?" Gino raised his voice. "How far is it to where we're going?"

"About fifteen minutes," the driver said. "Not far."

Something was bothering Gino. He frowned, and looked at the back of the chauffeur's head. "Say, you're a new driver, aren't you?"

"Yes, I am," Teddy Fay said.

AUTHOR'S NOTE

I am happy to hear from readers, but you should know that if you write to me in care of my publisher, three to six months will pass before I receive your letter, and when it finally arrives it will be one among many, and I will not be able to reply.

However, if you have access to the Internet, you may visit my website at www.stuartwoods.com, where there is a button for sending me e-mail. So far, I have been able to reply to all my e-mail, and I will continue to try to do so.

If you send me an e-mail and do not receive a reply, it is probably because you are among an alarming number of people who have entered their e-mail address incorrectly in their mail software. I have many of my replies returned as undeliverable.

Remember: e-mail, reply; snail mail, no reply.

When you e-mail, please do not send attachments, as I never open these. They can take twenty minutes to download, and they often contain viruses.

Please do not place me on your mailing lists for funny stories, prayers, political causes, charitable fund-raising, petitions, or sentimental claptrap. I get enough of that from people I already know. Generally speaking, when I get e-mail addressed to a large number of people, I immediately delete it without reading it.

Please do not send me your ideas for a book, as I have a policy of writing only what I myself invent. If you send me story ideas, I will immediately delete them without reading them. If you have a good idea for a book, write it yourself, but I will not be able to advise you on how to get it published. Buy a copy of **Writer's Market** at any bookstore; that will tell you how.

Anyone with a request concerning events or appearances may e-mail it to me or send it to: Publicity Department, Penguin Random House LLC, 1745 Broadway, New York, NY 10019.

Those ambitious folk who wish to buy film,

dramatic, or television rights to my books should contact Matthew Snyder, Creative Artists Agency, 2000 Avenue of the Stars, Los Angeles, CA 90067.

Those who wish to make offers for rights of a literary nature should contact Anne Sibbald, Janklow & Nesbit, 285 Madison Avenue, New York, NY 10017. (Note: This is not an invitation for you to send her your manuscript or to solicit her to be your agent.)

If you want to know if I will be signing books in your city, please visit my website, www.stuart woods.com, where the tour schedule will be published a month or so in advance. If you wish me to do a book signing in your locality, ask your favorite bookseller to contact his Penguin representative or the Penguin publicity department with the request.

If you find typographical or editorial errors in my book and feel an irresistible urge to tell someone, please write to Sara Minnich at Penguin's address above. Do not e-mail your discoveries to me, as I will already have learned about them from others.

A list of my published works appears in the front of this book and on my website. All the novels are still in print in paperback and can be found at or ordered from any bookstore. If you wish to obtain hardcover copies of earlier novels or of the two nonfiction books, a good used-book store or one of the online bookstores can help you find them. Otherwise, you will have to go to a great many garage sales.

STUART WOODS is the author of more than eighty novels. He is a native of Georgia and began his writing career in the advertising industry. **Chiefs,** his debut in 1981, won the Edgar Award. An avid sailor and pilot, Woods lives in Key West, Mount Desert Island, and Santa Fe.

STUARTWOODS.COM
FACEBOOK.COM/STUARTWOODSAUTHOR

PARNELL HALL is an actor, screenwriter, singer/songwriter, and the author of more than forty novels. He has received the Eye Lifetime Achievement Award from the Private Eye Writers of America, has won a Shamus Award, and has been a finalist for numerous other crime writing awards. Hall lives in New York City.

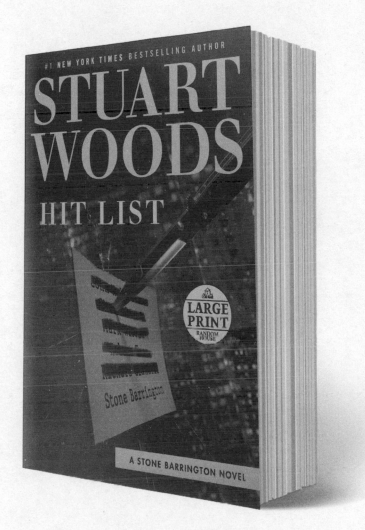